I0684355

Praise for Steve Lowe & THE FIX

"THE FIX floats like a butterfly and stings like a sledgehammer to the face. This fast-paced, loving homage to its crime fiction forefathers swings like pure pulp magic."

— Jeremy Robert Johnson, author of *Skullcrack City* and *We Live Inside You*

"Lowe is one of those authors who reinvents himself with each book and yet somehow maintains his voice intact." —*Verbicide*

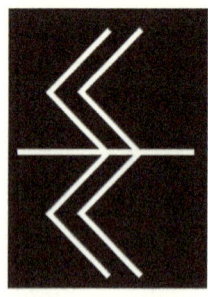

A Broken River Books original

Broken River Books
103 Beal Street
Norman, OK 73069

ISBN: 978-1-940885-11-7

Printed in the USA.

THE FIX

by
Steve Lowe

BROKEN RIVER BOOKS
NORMAN, OK

As always, as will be forever,
this is for Michele

THIS
MORNING

Nichols sat on the Caprice's bumper and pulled his boots from the open trunk. Not that his scuffed, off-the-rack Cole Haans were worth much, bought on sale at Nordstroms, but they were his only pair of dress shoes, and that's what the boots were for—walking through the muck of a crime scene. He tucked his slacks inside the ankle-high boots and walked across the street to the burned out shell of the body shop carrying a legal pad and pen. Had to hold the pad close to shield it from the water dripping off the blackened rafters overhead. He wished he'd thought to bring a different shirt, but too late for that now.

Hot spots smoldered and the building's corrugated metal cladding, expanded by the heat of the inferno, creaked loudly as it contracted, twisted into new shapes. Cargill, the medical examiner, waited for him in the middle of the charred mess. Nichols didn't bother to stop and look at the two bodies just outside the building. They were barely burned but filled with bullet holes, lying under sheets in the gutter. At the top of his note pad were their names:

Sims, Henry, 56, Caucasian male.
Dudek, Michael "Mick", 40, Caucasian male.

These two he knew. Shady characters, bookmakers. A dying breed in Chicago with the proliferation of Indian casinos and online sports books. Both dead as hell, and not from the explosion. Forensics already had more than a dozen 7.62 casings from the street. Somebody opened up on those boys with an assault rifle, two connected types ventilated by a machine gun. Just like in the good old days. That made Nichols smile. At least some things didn't change.

The four inside, he did not know. Not yet, not officially. He would soon enough, but for now, he had a few educated guesses. He picked his way through the tangled, burned mess on the floor until he stood next to Cargill, who said, "Hey, Ray."

"Find any ID on these guys yet?"

Cargill shook his head. "If they have ID on them, it's probably melted to their asses."

"Looks like arson?"

"That's not my call. I'll let the Cook County Arson Unit handle that."

"You see that over there by the door?"

Cargill looked and said, "What?"

Nichols pointed. "Look like a charcoal grill to you?"

"I don't know, could be."

"The blast definitely happened up front. Hunks of shrapnel from an oil drum all over the street out there. This place went up quick. Responding units said it was totally engulfed when they arrived on scene."

Cargill just nodded, looked vaguely interested. Nichols said, "What do we know about these crispy critters in here?"

Cargill pointed them out to Nichols. "We have a total of four. One right here on the floor, looks like this was the entrance to a back office. That right there is a desk. You have victim number two still sitting in a chair there, victim three on the floor in front of the desk, and victim four crouched down behind the desk. You can see his arm still stuck to the top? That's because somebody nailed it there with a spike."

"I'm guessing not his number one fan."

"Someone definitely had a beef with these guys. And I have a feeling the cause of death will not be from smoke inhalation."

Cargill crouched and gently lifted the first victim's scorched head, pointed with a pink-latex-gloved finger. "See that?"

"Big hole he's got there."

"The other three have one as well."

"I'd say that looks like something a three-fifty-seven would do to a skull."

Cargill nodded, gently set the corpse's head down. A uniformed officer out on the sidewalk called for Nichols.

"You find some neighbors willing to talk?"

The uniform looked around the demilitarized zone of a neighborhood and back at Nichols, who laughed and said, "Just kidding. What about the Cadillac parked up the street?"

"I tried. It's locked."

"But you have a key."

"I do?"

Nichols pointed at the officer's baton. "Hanging on your belt."

"You want me to break into the car?"

"No, the window blew in from the blast. You follow me?"

The officer thought about it a minute and said, "Yeah, I guess so."

"Get the registration out of the glove box. I want to know the dumbass who parks a brand new XTS in the middle of niggertown and leaves it."

The cop's face reddened as he headed off toward the Cadillac and Nichols wondered if the kid was angry or embarrassed by his hate speech. That phrase made him laugh, all the political correctness and bullshit these days. A second later, he heard the sound of breaking glass. Nichols grinned at Cargill, who said, "What's your guess they were shooting each other over? Money? Drugs? Both?"

"Probably I'd say money. If those two assholes out front were involved, my guess is it's a bet gone bad." His eyes flicked over to Cargill, waited for his reaction.

After a minute, Cargill said, "So if it's money, my guess is we're not going to find it in here anywhere."

"No, I don't suppose we will."

"Wasn't there a fight last night?"

"Yep."

"You watch it?"

"Nope."

"Not a boxing fan?"

"What was it Capone said in *The Untouchables*?" Nichols slipped into a bad DeNiro impression. "You

4

got an all-out prizefight, you wait until the fight's over, one guy is left standing. *That's* how you know who won.'"

Cargill looked around. "So who was left standing?"

"Good question."

Nichols picked his way through the mess, looked at each corpse a little closer. Faint smell of gas beneath the musk of barbequed flesh. The guy still sitting in the chair was probably welded to it. Nichols looked at the hole in his forehead, at the cooked lips curled away from yellow teeth. By his tally, everyone that was supposed to be there was accounted for, pending dental record confirmation. All of them were dead, and none of them had the money.

That meant somebody showed up who hadn't been expected. Find the party crasher, find the cash.

He nudged the corpse.

"What do say fella? Tell me a story. Who was left standing?"

PART I: MEAN RIGHT HOOK

Buster pulled the stall door closed behind him, sat on the stool, and placed his boots between his feet. He stopped for a second and listened, waited. Voices from up the hall, the last undercard getting ready to start. An entourage pumping their guy up, stuff in Spanish that Buster didn't understand, but knew intimately anyway.

You the man.

You got this.

Ain't no thing.

Punk bitch is goin' down.

Buster dropped them a year ago. Having your boys around helps some guys. Not Buster. He didn't need anybody around, just Uncle Mitch. All that other shit was distraction. Motherfuckers hanging on, trying to snag a piece of you. Suck the life out of you, drain you. Every hour of the fucking day, man.

That's what he told himself. That wasn't the real reason his boys stopped coming around. One thing a loser can spot is another loser. Rest is just talking up in your head with yourself. Rationalization was more abundant than reality these days.

Buster waited for the voices to trail away down the hall before he moved again.

Had to hurry.

He reached into his bag and pulled out his rig. Had it ready to go so he didn't have to fuck around with cooking right there in the bathroom. It was just one hit, a tenth of a gram, not a lot, but enough to get him through the fight.

It wasn't going past the fourth round, anyway.

Buster crossed his right leg on top of his left and tied off a length of rubber tubing just below the knee. He rubbed his calf down toward his ankle and slapped at the veins crisscrossing the top of his right foot. They popped up like fat worms under his skin. He didn't bother with the left foot anymore. Waste of time.

He hated doing the foot, but no way he could bang it into his arm. Can't get into the ring with tracks. Might as well paint that shit on your forehead in big ass letters.

Buster flicked the rig and poked it into the vein, worked it around, pulled it out, tried again. Nearly dropped it. Fingers stiff like burned sausages poking out of the layers of white medical tape. His foot hurt like hell and he stopped and leaned back against the toilet. Stared up at the ceiling. Listened to the crowd somewhere off in the distance. Boos, probably for the spic fighter. Puerto Rican dude, Buster couldn't remember his name, a welterweight. Good fighter. Buster watched him spar. Quick, lots of power behind his punches. He'd hit you three times before you threw one. Fight wouldn't go past round two. Buster had to hurry the fuck up.

"Come on, man."

He leaned forward and tried again, forced himself to slow down. Got it that time. Drew some blood into the murky brown mix, oily mud inside the rig. Sent it down, drove it in, leaned back again and felt it slide through him. Just needed a minute now. Just set there and wait, let it ride.

"Buster, the fuck is you doin' in here?"

Buster flinched, yanked the rig out of his foot. Balled up some toilet paper and blotted the hole in his vein. Flushed the toilet and grabbed his boots.

"Yeah," he said, tried hard not to slur his words. "Comin', man. Takin' a shit."

Uncle Mitch didn't say anything, just grunted. Buster waited for the door to click shut again and stuffed his works back in the bag, set about putting on his boots. Couldn't get his stiff fingers to lace them up right.

"Goddammit, come *on*, man."

He tried again, couldn't. Said *fuck it* and shoved out of the crapper, hustled back down the hall. Uncle Mitch stood next to the table, tapped Buster's gloves together. Motioned with his eyes to the corner. Buster looked.

"Buster, my man." Sonny sat on the bench in front of Buster's locker, hunched over, drumming on the worn wood between his legs. Playing some college fight song, tapping out the beat. Annoying motherfucker. His boy, Ricky, behind him, leaned up against the lockers, about a foot taller than any of them. Head practically scraping the low-hanging pipes and ductwork in the ceiling. Ricky didn't look at him. Stared at his fingers, picked at the nails, like he couldn't be more bored. But he was watching. Buster knew better.

"Mr. Porter." Buster looked at Uncle Mitch, real quick, back to Sonny. "Want to thank you for settin' this fight up."

Sonny looked down and laughed, shook his head. Stood up and swung his leg over the bench and walked up to Buster. He looked down at the bag in Buster's right hand. Arched his eyebrows. Patted Buster on the shoulder and said, "I come to wish you good luck in tonight's contest."

Sonny smiled and Ricky crowded in on the other side of Buster.

Sonny said, "So, good luck in tonight's contest."

"Thank you. 'Preciate it."

Sonny nodded and headed for the door, Ricky a step behind. They passed into the hall and Buster looked over his shoulder, watched them go. Sonny turned back, smile still plastered on. He held up his right hand and flashed four fingers at Buster. Turned his hand around to show him front and back. Buster just watched, waited for them to go, for the door to swing shut. He looked back at Mitch. The old man's face was blank. Stared him down. The crowd up the tunnel jeered, booed the lightning fast little Puerto Rican carving up their neighborhood boy. Almost done out there. Main event up next.

Mitch blinked first. He looked down at Buster's boots, at the untied laces. Shook his head. His shoulders dropped, almost imperceptible. He set the gloves on the table and shuffled over to cinch the laces up for Buster.

They didn't exchange a word while Uncle Mitch knotted the boots and moved on to the gloves. Buster looked at him until his uncle finally met his eyes. Buster saw the hurt there. Knew what he was doing to the old man, who raised him up from a boy when his own father wouldn't. Taught him how to fight. Showed him everything. Killing him with this shit and Buster knew it. But it was too late to think about that. Because this shit was already in motion. No turning back now.

"Uncle Mitch, it'll be alright. I got this."

Mitch read his eyes, looking at one back to the other. Buster wondered if they were bloodshot, figured they probably were by the pained expression on Mitch's face. The old man always was smarter than he wanted you to think.

"Is you stupid? What're you doin' fooling around with this mess?"

Buster looked down at his gloves, couldn't bear up under that gaze any longer. Breaking his uncle's heart was what he was doing, but he was doing it anyhow.

Mitch grunted, shook his head.

"I'd like to say I hope you know what you doin', but I already know that you don't." He pulled hard on the laces, biting into Buster's wrists. He barely felt it.

Out in the hall: loud voices, shouting and singing in Spanish. The Puerto Rican was done. A minute later there was a knock at their door and a head poked in, said, "Alright y'all, time to go."

Mitch walked to the door, went through. Didn't wait for Buster. He sat there another second, sweating already, drenched. Heart thumping against his ribs. Numb and mad, getting madder. For what he was

13

doing to Mitch. For what he was doing to himself. For what was going to happen in that ring. He smacked his gloves together and hopped off the table, jogged up the tunnel after his uncle.

Buster hardly heard the intros, just zoned out and bounced around, tried to get loose, throw a couple uppercuts when the guy sings your name out and then get through the ref's spiel about low blows and stay on your toes. Buster didn't even bother to touch gloves, just turned and walked to his corner. That drew a lusty jeer from the crowd, which he hardly heard.

He shuffled in his corner waiting for the bell. He wiggled his arms, bounced from foot to foot, up on his toes. Tried to be loose but it wasn't working. That first shot will get him going. Always did. One good smack to his jaw got him into a fight. Endorphins and shit wake you up. He waited for Mitch to say something but he just stood there, looking over his shoulder at Buster's opponent, Ronnie Piccolo.

He shook his head and said to Buster, "You used to spar this fool. Now you gonna take a dive for him."

"Ain't like that, Uncle Mitch."

"Bullshit it ain't. What is it then?"

Buster watched Ronnie who watched him back. Smug sneer on his face. Buster looked out at the crowd, found Sonny and Ricky two rows away from ringside. Sonny on his cellphone, smiled and gave him a thumbs-up when they made eye contact.

The referee pointed to both corners and then at the timekeeper at ringside. Mitch shoved Buster's mouth guard in and climbed through the ropes as the bell rang for the fight to start.

14

Buster slide-stepped forward, hands up. Ronnie Piccolo sauntered out of his corner, hands near his waist. Buster had to bite the inside of his cheek to keep from dropping that fool right then. A buzz in the crowd when he cocked back that right hand of his, like they saw it coming too, just waiting for a Buster overhand right to destroy Ronnie Piccolo eleven seconds into the fight. He threw a left jab instead and went for the body. Tied the prick up and leaned into his ear and said, "Stop prancing around and fight you faggot."

He pushed Ronnie away and skipped back, rolled his head around on his neck but couldn't feel it. He was still too stiff, felt like a wooden board out there. He needed that first punch, craved it like a loaded rig. Ronnie's cheeks burned and he stepped in with a wild right hook that Buster didn't bother to block. The punch was weak and he knew that tomato can would never be able to knock him out for real, probably wear himself down trying. Everybody packed around that ring knew it too, that Buster had more talent and power is his right hand alone than a dozen bums like Ronnie Piccolo put together. And that was the problem. Only one didn't seem to give a shit was Sonny Porter.

Ronnie caught Buster with an uppercut that loosed bees in his ears. Buster danced back, shook his head, and just like that, his whole body went fluid. Flip of a switch and the electrodes clamped on his muscles let go. Now he could fight. But he didn't, not just yet. He finished the round with three punches thrown. The bell rang and he walked back to his corner.

Mitch offered him the water bottle and he swished some in his mouth, spat pink into his bucket. Buster looked around for Sonny Porter while Mitch smeared Vaseline on his cheeks. The old man didn't say a word because he knew there was no point. Buster could beat this bum with his eyes closed. Mitch didn't need to tell him that, so he didn't. Just grabbed the bucket and the stool and slipped back between the ropes.

Buster looked at Sonny just as the bell rang for the second round. Sonny cocked his head and put up his dukes, threw a couple shadow punches at Buster. Telling him to do something out there, make it look good. Sonny didn't understand that the only way to make this look good was for Buster to flatten Ronnie right then. Anything less and everybody in the state of Illinois would know the fix was in. And that wouldn't just be Sonny's problem, but Buster's, too.

He split Ronnie's lip with two fast left jabs but kept the right put away like it was belted down to his side. Ronnie was already getting tired, dropping his hands and not on purpose anymore. Buster burned with embarrassment because he did nothing about it. Just danced and jabbed and locked up with the flabby breadstick until the bell rang.

This time, Mitch did talk to him.

"Ain't you got no pride?"

Buster didn't answer. He watched Ronnie, but Ronnie looked down at the mat while his man worked on his busted lip. He already looked beat and they had one more round to get through.

"Ain't you embarrassed?"

Buster looked at Sonny Porter, who smiled and golf-clapped for him.

Mitch grabbed Buster's chin and pulled his face around, got nose to nose with him.

"Godammit, Tyrone, don't you disrespect me like that. When I speak to you son, you damn well better look me in the eyes."

Buster nodded, said, "Yessir."

"Well? What you got to say to me?"

Buster had nothing to say to his uncle. The bell rang and he slid past the old man. He spent the third round in Ronnie's ear.

"Come on, bitch," he said. "Show the folks something. They expecting you to put on a show. Ain't you got nothing for them? Bet if this was the shower in Stateville you be fighting for me. You put up a fight for that ass, wouldn't ya?"

Ronnie gave him a flurry and Buster absorbed it, stored it, saved it for later. When Ronnie slowed, Buster shoved him back and caught him with a straight right that detonated Ronnie's nose. He staggered back but stayed on his feet. The crowd jumped to its feet at the sight of blood and clamored for more, for Buster to finish it.

Buster just bounced in place and waited for him. Ronnie wiped at his face, looked at the blood smeared across his glove. He didn't get any closer than he had to until the bell rang. Boos from the crowd. Round three over. Round four up next. Somebody chucked a water bottle into the ring that burst and sprayed the judges. The announcer hollered at the crowd to settle down. The crowd hollered back that they didn't come to see this shit. They weren't mad at Ronnie, either. Something heavy like a D battery struck Buster in the back, but he didn't look around or give it back to the crowd. He knew he deserved it.

Buster watched Sonny as he stood in his corner. Sonny held four fingers to his chest and looked from Buster to Ronnie, both of them watching him. Buster dropped onto his stool and looked across at Ronnie. Surprised as hell. Prick wasn't expecting to have his nose bent over like that. He looked scared. Buster grinned and winked at him.

He said to Mitch, "Promise me something."

Mitch stopped sponging water on his head and looked at him.

"What?"

"Don't go back for your stuff. Leave it. Just head up that east tunnel and go out the back, by the dumpsters. Go out the emergency exit. Catch a cab and leave out. Don't wait for me or nothin' because I won't be there, and you don't want to be neither."

Mitch watched him for a second then looked around the arena until he spotted Sonny and Ricky. Sonny waved at them with four fingers.

"Son, you gonna get yourself killed."

"Ain't nobody getting killed 'cept that piece of shit across the way. You just do what I told you and light out of here with the quickness. Don't hang around to see. They'll follow me, you just go the other way."

The bell rang for round four and Buster sprang up, stalked to the center of the ring. Ronnie shuffled forward, unsure. He gave Sonny one more look and moved in with an overhand right. Buster turned away from it, let the blow bounce off his shoulder. Brought his right arm back, like packing ball and powder down the barrel of a cannon, loaded up and set his feet in the same motion. He threw his first real right hand of the fight and blew Ronnie Piccolo to pieces. The hook caught Ronnie flush on the left temple and snapped his head nearly all the way around so he could look back at his corner. The last thing he would see.

The fist, the right hand of Buster Grant, was a thing of beauty. What every person in that building save two were waiting to see. What brought them out to the south side of Chicago that night and brought them to their feet right then. The building exploded, the sound of Buster's right fist connecting, the crack of bone snapping, the slap of Ronnie's face slamming into the canvas.

The ref didn't bother to count. He waved the doctor into the ring because he heard it just as well as everyone else. The ring instantly filled with people. Buster lost sight of Sonny and Ricky in the chaos, a sea of madness inside the ring and out. The crowd gone out of their minds over what they just saw. Fights broke out among the seats, maybe for no other reason than the pure, visceral energy of watching one man destroy another. It was too much to process, just trigger the collective bloodlust.

Buster lost sight of his uncle as well. The ref barely got his right hand up in the air to signal him the winner than Buster shoved through the bodies and the ropes and fought his way through the throng for the west exit. Congratulatory slaps but also a few angry fists pounded him, bettors probably aware of the fix and unhappy with a result counter to what they had been promised. Buster smiled at these, gave a couple shots back for the fun of it. The place was devolving into an all-out riot and Buster had to punch his way out. One shot that burst open a fat white guy's face did the trick. The false warriors, showered by a friend's blood, created a bubble around Buster, allowing him to pass to the exit.

Buster shoved through the doors amid a horde of people streaming for safe haven from the chaos. He moved up Halsey Street and cut down an alley, crossed over four blocks to Carter where the cab was waiting for him. He tapped the back window with his glove and waited for the driver to unlock the door.

The driver looked back at Buster, took in his getup and seemed to figure out the situation pretty quick.

"Hey, brother, I ain't looking to get into nothing here."

"Too late, you already in something. And I ain't your brother."

"No way man, this wasn't part of the deal."

Buster grabbed the front seat with his right glove, slick with the fat man's blood. "You don't get your ass moving right now, you're gonna get a whole lot more than you bargained for, you feel me?"

He looked at the bloody boxing glove, Buster's wild, bloodshot eyes, turned and grabbed the wheel. While he drove, Buster worked at the laces of his left glove with his teeth.

"You never said where I was taking you."

"Don't worry about it yet, you're already heading in the right direction."

They drove several minutes in silence, Buster chewing at his glove, the driver watching him in the mirror.

"Take a right up here," Buster said.

The driver did as he was told. Buster finally worked the left glove off, tossed it out the window. He reached into his trunks and said, "Up on the right, the body shop."

The driver stopped at the curb. Buster peeled the sweaty bill from his crotch and handed it across the seat. The driver took it between the tips of two fingers, made a face.

"What the hell is this?"

"That's one hundred dollars like we agreed."

"Man, I'm not taking this. It was down your drawers."

Buster opened the door, stepped out. "Then don't take it. Up to you."

The driver shook his head and laid the sodden bill on the seat next to him. Squealed his tires a bit as he took off. Buster stood in darkness under the metal awning over the front door to the shop. He watched the street for several minutes, picked at the laces of his right glove. Satisfied no one was around, he bent and lifted a broken corner of the sidewalk in front of the shop, dug out the key hidden there, let the concrete fall back in place.

Buster stuck his right glove under his left arm, pulled it from his hand, yanked the padlock and chain from the door handles and shoved inside. He shut the door behind him and noticed a light on in the back office. He knew he hadn't left it on. Didn't bother to

21

investigate, just turned and pushed back out the front door, but ran face first into something heavy, swung out from the shadows.

Buster opened his eyes and saw the ceiling of the shop above him. Coughed and turned his head to spit out a mouthful of hot soup. It was thick and red and filled with cracked teeth. Laid his pounding head back on the floor and looked up at the ceiling again. Heard the front door latch close. Overhead lights flickered on, buzzed like flies. A face loomed over his. Two faces. Ricky, hefting a pipe wrench in his hand, slapping it in his palm. And Sonny, bent over and smiling. His lips moved but Buster couldn't hear anything at first. Began to fade. He jerked awake when Sonny squeezed his shattered mouth.

"Hey, there you are. Thought we were losing you."

Buster tried to speak, choked on the blood pooling in the back of his throat.

Sonny said, "I was telling you that I'm impressed. You guys had a pretty good plan. But you had one problem. I saw that movie, too."

Buster blacked out after that.

When Buster woke up, it took a few minutes to gain his bearings. He was in a chair, strapped down with duct tape. From his ankles to his knees, broad spans of it across his thighs. Stuck to the bare skin of his belly and chest, looping around the chair, him, his left arm pinned to his side. The only thing not covered with broad bands of silver tape was his head and right arm. His head bowed forward as far as his taped-down torso would allow. A thick rope of red drool hung from his wrecked mouth, all the way to the floor between his boots. A bloody tether, the only thing still holding him to the earth.

Metallic snap of a lighter cover, spin of a wheel rubbed against flint, snick of ignition. With great effort, Buster nudged his head up enough that he might look at the source of that sound. He was careful not to snap the drool lest he spin flying off into hell. But probably, he was already there.

"Hey, Buster." Sonny Porter sat across from him, on the other side of a battered metal desk. It was the desk in the back office at the body shop. Buster glanced around and confirmed his location. On the desk between them, Sonny had laid out Buster's works, lined up and uniform, like a priest's baptismal implements.

The Zippo lighter stood in the center, the flame wobbling. Sonny picked up the spoon, slow and reverent, giving the ceremony its deserving respect. He tapped out half a gram of brown granules into the spoon. Big hit, much more than Buster would normally bang. Enough to last him a whole week. He admitted his addiction, but he still retained the frugal nature his Uncle Mitch had tried to instill in him. Maybe the only thing he had left.

Buster didn't move, just watched Sonny cook. He placed the spoon over the flame and waited for it to boil. Set it on the desk and blotted it with a cotton ball. Stuck the end of a fresh needle into the cotton, drew up the dirty liquid. Held it up for both of them to stare in wonder at the slow-swirling mixture inside. Buster tracked the needle with his eyes and snapped his tether. He didn't notice.

Sonny looked around the syringe so Buster could see his eyes. "What happens from here on out depends on how this goes."

He raised his eyebrows expectantly. Buster nodded, more blood and slobber spilling out between his battered, swollen lips. He saw a flashback of the pipe wrench streaking out of the shadows, felt it bite into his face, mash his teeth into the back of his mouth. He flinched and looked around for Ricky. The big man wasn't there.

"Just you and me for the moment," Sonny said. He got up and walked around the desk, plucked the yellow tubing up in his hand as he moved behind Buster. He watched and waited a moment. Buster flopped his right arm up on the desk, turned his palm toward the ceiling. He had no intention of fighting Sonny. He was smart enough to know when he was beat. And at this point, he wanted that hit. Wanted it bad.

Sonny saw this and moved closer. Wrapped the tubing around Buster's right arm just above the elbow, cinched it down tight. The veins leapt up under his skin. The sight of them made his heart skip. Perfect, untouched vessels that he'd had actual dreams about, stabbing that needle into something other than his goddamn foot. He was ready for it now. Anything to take away the banjo-strum ache in his mouth. The shame of this night. Tears rolled down his cheeks.

Sonny picked up the rig and held it to the light, flicked the air bubbles to the top, gave the plunger a squeeze until a bead of liquid dribbled from the needle.

"Hey, you know what you doing, man?" A gush of stringy blood spilled down Buster's front with each word.

Sonny said nothing as he leaned over the desk, slapped at Buster's skin, rubbed the bulging veins snaking up his forearm. Plenty to choose from. Sonny picked out a fat one just inside the elbow. Buster tilted his arm to accommodate him. Sonny opened an alcohol wipe with his teeth and rubbed it over the vein. He held the rig between his thumb and forefinger, poked it into the vein at an angle, smooth and gentle. It popped right in on the first try. They both smiled reflexively, happy with the result. Sonny drew back the plunger, sucked in some thick blood. They both watched it for a second, mesmerized by the suspended red glob. Sonny didn't push it in right away.

"You're going to tell me who set up your bet."

Buster's eyes flicked up from the rig in his arm to Sonny. He nodded quick, flopping strings of drool from his lips. Sonny's gaze remained locked into Buster's as he banged the hit home. The effect was much faster and much harder than shooting into his foot. Near instantaneous. He couldn't keep his eyelids up. Sonny withdrew the empty rig but Buster barely noticed, hardly heard him say, "You enjoy that for a bit and I'll be back later to talk."

Buster sat in the chair, his slack arm still extended across the metal desk, for what could have been minutes or hours. He didn't know and he didn't give a shit.

Sonny came back later. Buster was in and out of reality until a bucket of icy water hit his face.

"Whew!" Sonny pinched his nose. "Buster, did you shit yourself? I think you did."

Buster didn't know but believed it. His face felt like it was filled with lead but the pain was mostly gone. Not entirely, but receded, crawled up deep into his brain like a dead appendage. Coiled away like a rattlesnake.

His arm was still on the table, limp, palm turned up, but Buster noted with something approaching amusement that his boxing glove was on again. The laces remained loose, like somebody just shoved it on and kept about their business. He was certain he had taken it off when he got to the shop.

Sonny snapped his fingers in Buster's face. They blurred as they floated through the air. "Buster, yo. Can you hear me, homeboy?"

Buster spit between his feet. "I can hear ya. I ain't your homeboy."

"I'm sorry. That was a little racist, wasn't it? I'll try to do better."

Sonny walked around the desk, sat down in the other metal chair. Propped his hand on something, looked to Buster like a wood handle. Smell of smoke somewhere, something burning. He didn't know if it was real.

"Congratulations on the fight tonight," Sonny said. "The right hook of yours, boy." Sonny shook his head, grinning. "Goddamn, son. Best right hook I think I've ever seen in person. It's too bad."

"What's too bad?" Sonny wobbled in Buster's vision and he moved his arm back, tried to sit straight.

"Do me a favor and just keep your arm on top of the desk where I can see it, OK?"

Buster slid his hand back, propped his unstable head against his shoulder. Too high to realize it had gone to sleep and would be useless to him anyway.

"Too bad because of what has to happen next. You know what has to happen next, don't you?"

Buster did and bobbed his head.

"Buster, raw talent-wise, you might be the best boxer for whom I have ever had the pleasure of promoting a fight. I sincerely mean that. You should have been fighting for a belt by now, and probably should be wearing at least one of them. But you've wasted that talent."

Sonny picked Buster's bag up off the floor, pulled all his works out again and laid it on the desktop. "You wasted it on this stuff. And now your career is over. A damn shame."

Buster tried to say, *Fuck you*, drooled over his arm instead.

"You're sick," Sonny said. "You are unwell. That's the only reason why I'm going to give you an option here."

He concentrated, forced the words out this time. "Just kill me and go fuck yourself."

"I'm not going to kill you, Buster. Do you prefer Tyrone or Buster? All this time I've never even thought to ask you that. I assumed since everyone called you Buster, that's what you liked best, but Tyrone is a good name as well."

Buster didn't answer, just mumbled into his shoulder, tried to look around the room. Everything spun, the world a pinwheel. He vomited into his lap.

"No, I'm not going to kill you, though you are going to have to make a choice. But I'll tell you about that in a bit, after it gets here. First, I wanted to thank you."

"For what?"

"For coming through tonight. I had you pegged from the start and you didn't let me down."

Buster forced himself to lock in on Sonny, keep him in the center of his vision instead of rolling away. He was about to ask what Sonny meant by that when it struck him. "You didn't bet on Ronnie."

"No, I did not."

"You never meant to bet on Ronnie, did you?"

Sonny shook his head, smiled.

"You had me set up from the beginning. Played me like a goddamn fool."

"I didn't play you, Buster. I just knew you well enough to know what you would do. Call it intuition on my part, though I did also have experience on my side here, too. That's a story for another day, though. They only thing I didn't know is, who you fell in with to put up your bet. I'll find that out soon enough, but I've got my ideas."

Buster laid his head on his shoulder again and closed his eyes. "Played me like the damn fool I am." He laughed, thick and wet with blood and puke and phlegm.

"If you were thinking clearly, you would have known your bet never would have gone through on its own. That's the problem with this shit." Sonny picked up the baggie, the last remaining bit of Buster's dope. "Your mind is unclear when you use this. You make poorly informed decisions. You associate with the wrong crowd. It's bad news."

Somewhere behind Buster, echoes from the end of a long, dark tunnel, a door banged shut. Sonny looked up at the office door, said, "Yes?" to someone there. A body passed into the room, a shadow crossed over Buster's face. He looked up at Ricky, canted sideways with Buster's head still across his shoulder. Ricky placed a leather bag on the desk and looked down at Buster.

"You are one filthy fuckin' nigger," he said to Buster.

Sonny handed the bucket across the desk to Ricky. "Do me a favor and fill that up again for me, would you?"

Ricky grabbed the bucket without looking, kept his contemptible glare focused on Buster. Buster tried to spit on him but couldn't tell where the projectile landed. Probably all over himself. Sonny tapped his boxing-gloved right hand and showed Buster the satchel, held it open for him to see the money inside.

"There's your winning bet, dog. This is as close as you'll ever get to it."

Buster sneered and looked away at the wall. "But you ain't gonna kill me?"

"No, I am not going to kill you. But I assure you, your boxing days are over."

"What you gonna do then?"

Sonny closed the satchel, set it on the floor behind the desk, returned his hand to the top of the upright wooden handle. "That's what I need to talk to you about. You see, I'm trying to run a business here. I have ambitions, which go beyond the relatively low ceiling of boxing promotions. In fact, I'm moving away from that end of it altogether, mainly because I'm tired of dealing with this sort of thing. Your admittedly honorable attempt to circumvent my authority is a major issue for me. I informed some rather important investors and gaming enthusiasts that the outcome of your bout was known ahead of time and that they could place their wagers with the utmost confidence in me, that it was an ironclad certainty. And now their confidence in me is shaken, likely for good. At this moment, my own future is in question. I took that into consideration when I originally arranged this fight and decided that if I were to allow you to go ahead with your plans, I would be required afterword to make a grand showing on my investors' behalf in an attempt to save face with them."

"You keeping my money, ain't you?"

Sonny laughed, said, "You're not the sharpest knife in the drawer, are you?" Then his face was serious. "It never was your money, Buster. Your bet never goes through without me. The way the line moved right before the fight throws up red flags, but only for those not in on the fix. They don't want to get caught with their thumbs up their collective asses, so their antennas are suddenly up, and then when your bet comes in five minutes before the fight, they notice it. They're already looking, and this just stands out to them like a beacon in the dark. I knew who you were using and I was waiting for the call. Without my approval, the bet would have been rejected. I told them to let it go. That poses different problems, but those are uptown problems for me to deal with later."

Buster thought of the fight, right before the bell, Sonny on his cellphone. Knew the whole damn time. Just waiting for Buster to do what he knew from the get go Buster would do.

"But the price for this is I keep the winnings. A nice little pile of cash, I might add. So the deed is done and it cannot be un. And as a result, another bill has come due and must be paid. Do you see?"

Buster did, but didn't bother to acknowledge it. Only thing he cared about was the price. He shrieked and jerked his head back when the bucket of freezing water rushed over him. Zapped him up out of his heroin murk a bit, but not much. He was still buzzing nicely, all the pain and despair from the night's revelations remaining in the background. A concern for another day, not now. He didn't even flinch when Sonny stood and hefted the sledgehammer off the floor.

"The only thing I don't know for sure is who backed you. Guy like you, Buster, doesn't hatch this on his own. And as much of that shit you been flushing through your veins, I know you didn't have the capital to lay down a bet like that yourself. The way I figure, you come back here, gather your affects, wait for your cash, even up with your backer, and then ride off into the sunset. Am I close?"

Buster nodded.

"And I suppose you aren't going to just tell me who it is. Are you?"

Buster said nothing, which Sonny took as affirmation.

"That's fine. I'll know soon enough. We'll just wait here for your friend to show and give him his payoff. Boy will he be surprised!"

Ricky laughed, somewhere behind Buster.

"But in the meantime, I'll take from you what you owe me."

Ricky jumped on Buster, wrapped him up in a half-nelson, a heavy meathook under his right arm, snaked up behind his head. Ricky's left arm shoved up under Buster's chin, left hand grasping Buster's bicep. Buster didn't fight at first, the realization slow in coming. Swimming through the swamp of H in his brain.

"Unfortunately, I've had to do this before," Sonny said as he swung the sledge up and rested it across his shoulder. "I find it to be an effective display of what happens if someone conducts business with me in bad faith."

Sonny's face contorted, scrunched into an animal snarl. He brought the sledge down hard and fast, mashed the clean red boxing glove and Buster's hand inside. All the pain and torment languishing in the periphery of Buster's mind exploded through the swamp behind his forehead in a nuclear blast of agony. Like his hand detonated inside the glove. He swooned, darkness around the edges of his vision. Felt like he was going to puke again, the pain so sudden and real.

Sonny straightened and shouldered the sledge. Fixed his hair and mopped sweat from his upper lip with his jacket sleeve. "That's what the last guy got. Most of the bones in his hands were crushed. He never boxed again. Can't hardly use that hand for much anymore is what I hear. But he got the message. I thought everyone else did, too. But apparently, that wasn't enough, because here I am, back in this same situation once more, having to teach the same lesson over again."

He stepped back and swung the sledgehammer a second time, harder. It rebounded off the metal desk, off Buster's pulverized hand, nearly caught Sonny in the face. He said, "Whoa," and smiled, but his eyes were on Ricky, not Buster. They shared a laugh, two workingmen appreciating the hazards of their profession. He loosened his tie and set the sledge down, pulled his jacket off and placed it on the back of his chair. Dark sweat rings stained the armpits of his expensive pink dress shirt. He unbuttoned the cuffs, pure white like the collar, and rolled them up his forearms.

"I'm wondering now," Sonny said, panting, "what will be enough."

He shrugged and grabbed the sledgehammer again, swung it with enraged violence, made sure to dodge the rebound this time. The pain reached and then passed full bloom. Buster was on the down side now, slipping toward blackout.

"All those influential people who placed their trust in me and ended up losing money, they'll want me to kill you, but what good would that do? Once you're gone, everyone will forget. You'll pass out of their memories, and then before you know it, someone will try it again, and what good was the lesson then?"

Another heft, swing, smash. An audible splat from the glove, flatter now, its padding deflated. Bones inside just small pieces, ground to meal. Buster's arm was nearly numb, a combination of the heroin and a lack of circulation caused by Ricky's sleeper hold. A small mercy.

"Clearly, my previous example hadn't been adamant enough."

Sweat flew from Sonny's forehead as he swung the sledgehammer again, smashed Buster's right hand again. A crack bounced off the cheap paneling inside the office. Buster wondered if it was his hand breaking some more, or if the desk was giving way. He welcomed the darkness, wished it on quicker.

"As you can see, I have chosen a bolder course of action this time."

Sonny swung the sledgehammer again and again and again, hammering Buster's right hand until the glove was ruined and near to flat, the seams split and leaking blood. Sonny's fine dress shirt was sprinkled with dark dots, a spray of crimson ink. More splotches on his face as well. He flung the sledgehammer away into wall where it smashed a hole in the paneling. He plopped down in the chair, spent. He watched Buster, panted, dripped sweat. Inspected the mess on the desk.

Finally, Sonny looked at Ricky and nodded, tossed his chin toward the door.

Ricky let Buster go and left the office. Buster slumped against his shoulder, numb like it was no longer attached to his body. He didn't dare move his hand, if he even could. Tears streamed down his cheeks. Wished he would just pass out already, go away from that place, leave it behind.

Ricky returned to the office, set something down on the floor next to Buster with a heavy clunk. Handed another implement across the desk to Sonny, who stood and took a deep breath. Smell of burning stronger. Buster wanted to look but couldn't muster the strength to move his head. Ricky resumed his hold, but without the same intensity. Like he knew Buster was through.

"I know you won't want to hear this," Sonny said, low and close to Buster's ear. "But we're not done yet. You will be an example for folks to point to for a long time to come, Tyrone."

Sonny stepped back and lined the axe up where Buster's wrist met his hand. He rubbed a mark in the tape still there, lifted the axe high, brought it down slow, laid it on the mark. He lifted high again and brought it down hard. The head bit halfway through Buster's wrist, stopped cold when it hit the top of the radius bone. The shattering of that bone awoke the nerves throughout Buster's arm, the eruption of this new pain exceeding everything he just experienced. He screamed in agony for the first time, didn't stop screaming as Sonny hefted and chopped and hefted and chopped. Four whacks with the axe before he finally made it through and buried the axe head in the desktop.

Buster snapped back, tried to draw his ruined arm into his body, but Ricky gripped it between his hands and forced it down. Sonny stood at his side, the water bucket in hand, no longer filled with icy water, but with glowing, orange charcoals. Ricky held him down and Sonny drew the pail up. Blood streamed from Buster's wrist, splashing and hissing into the coals.

The darkness finally came and he was glad for it.

A COUPLE WEEKS AGO

Sims got into the car, made a show of himself, how hot it was outside. Fanned his face, red and sweaty.

"Ray, how are things?"

Nichols just nodded, didn't say anything. Made him sick to even be sitting next to this asshole, let alone him using his first name. Like they're friends.

"So," Sims said as he dabbed the sweat from his forehead with a handkerchief. "Let me guess. You don't have the money."

"Yet. I will." Soon as he said it, Nichols wished he hadn't. That's what every fucking deadbeat in history says, one time or another. It's what he got for laying money on the Brewers and that piece of shit Braun.

"Right, right. No, I understand, trust me."

Smug son of a bitch. Nichols wanted to just plug him right there and leave town. Don't give the guy the satisfaction of putting him through the ringer like this. Use the .25 strapped to his ankle. Belonged to a dead Haitian who tried to rob a liquor store in Little Italy and walked out with a twelve-gauge hole blown through him. Stupid little fuck didn't even get it out of his pocket before the shop owner blasted him. The .25 never showed up in Nichols' report. He could pull it out, stick it in this prick's ear, angle it toward the roof so the bullet didn't come out the other ear. Scramble his brains for him, shove him out the door down some alley.

He didn't. Just daydreaming.

"Look, don't give me this shit," Nichols said. "I'm not one of your goddamn deadbeats, alright? You'll have it. I just need a couple more days."

Sims nodded. He said, "That's fine. You pay me when you can. It's a lot of money."

Twisting the knife a little more. Digging it in. Nichols waited for him to get out, but Sims just kept nodding, staring out the windshield at the dark-haired kids throwing a tennis ball back and forth across the street, over the tops of the passing cars.

"Something else?"

"Yeah, one more thing." Sims opened his door, stuck one foot out onto the sidewalk, leaned closer to Nichols. "Should something... unforeseen happen, a package will show up at your precinct. There's some stuff inside that package. Well, copies of stuff actually, no originals. You know, receipts, maybe some photographs. You follow?"

Nichols watched a chubby Hispanic kid throw the ball, skip it off the roof of a passing Hyundai. "I follow."

"My nephew, the alderman, he'll make sure it gets where it needs to go."

Sims got out, shut the door. Stood on the sidewalk and waved at Nichols as he drove off. The tennis ball smacked into the passenger window as he drove by, but he kept going. He didn't even look at the fat kid.

Ten minutes later, he was sitting under a low-hanging tree, watching the back stairs of a crumbling two-story walkup in West Woodlawn. While he waited, he thought about Sims. The way the prick thought he could just casually threaten him like that. Getting Sims his money would not be a problem. Nichols wasn't even the slightest bit concerned about that. He was concerned with the alderman, though. That little shitheel, if he really did have copies of everything, gambling receipts and the like, would be a major issue.

Nichols grabbed his camera, a Nikon N70 SLR, used but still in great shape, out of a bag behind the driver's seat. He still used 35mm, mainly because he preferred the old fashioned way of doing things, but also because he learned to like the smell of the fixer. He appreciated the act of bringing a photo to life. He loved he technical side of real photography, knowing the how and not just the what.

Nichols enjoyed a good darkroom.

The guy he was waiting for showed up. Tall, broad, pale, the guy looked like a glow stick in this neighborhood. The dude glanced around quick before he took the stairs two at a time. Banged on a door covered in peeling green paint and a black guy answered, smiled and slapped him five, some ghetto handshake. He let the white guy in.

Nichols watched the lone window on the back of the house through a telescopic lens. He sat in the sticky stillness of the Caprice and smoked cigarettes and drank Diet Sprite and waited another fifteen minutes for the sun to go all the way down. When dusk was finally giving way to dark, he removed the big lens, slung the camera over his shoulder and walked across the street. The yard behind the building had a fence, but the rear stretch was gone, whatever the scrappers moving up and down the alleys could yank away from it as they cruised by. Same reason none of the garages that lined the alley had aluminum siding anymore.

Nichols waited at the bottom of the back steps and looked around the corner. Thunder cracked close by, a summer pop-up storm flaring overhead. That would keep the bangers off the streets for a while, leave Nichols to do his work in peace. Thankful for small miracles, he made his way up the steps. Music thumped in the upstairs apartment. The party had started.

He watched through the grease-streaked window, the two guys, one white, one black, leaned over a kitchen table, sucking coke into their faces, one line at a time. Heads bobbing to the music, Otis Redding. At least they had taste. The white guy leaned back, wiped at his nose, drained a Miller High Life. The black guy did the same then reached down and undid his pants. Let them slip down to his ankles. The white guy smiled and slid off his chair, onto his knees.

Nichols brought the camera up to the window, made sure the flash was off. He snapped away and was heading for his car five minutes later, just as the rain began to slap against the sidewalk. He figured he had almost two dozen clear shots of Ricky with some jigaboo's big, black dick in his mouth. Getting Sims his fucking money would be no trouble at all.

PART II:
OLD FRIENDS,
BAD PENNIES

Jimmy ignored the clock, just kept nailing. Stare at the clock too much and time slows down. So does your output. Can't make money on piece rate by watching the clock. He laid out the next piece of trim, double-checked that the cut lined up right in the corner, and slammed in the first nail. It took him about a week to get comfortable with the heft of the pneumatic finish nailer in his left hand, but his rates were already creeping up close to some of the senior production employees' numbers. They noticed that, too.

He didn't talk to anyone without first being talked to. Anti-social? Maybe. He preferred to keep his head down, keep focused on his job and his purpose for even being there. The more focused he was, the fewer mistakes he made, and on that job, every nail he shot came out of his paycheck. Every piece of trim that the assholes from QC pried off was a hit on his bottom line. The ones who talked a lot were the ones who took home less and bitched their lives away about it. Jimmy needed money, not friends. He'd had his fill of those.

He reached a near-meditative state of concentration, shooting those trim pieces in place. Floorboards, around the windows, interior and exterior, snapping his fingers for the laborer to keep up with him, hand him the correct piece. Slap on the last one and head down the line to the next unit. Don't get distracted, don't stop to bullshit. Before you know it, the buzzer sounds and it's lunchtime.

A queue formed at the tool cage, a supply room made of metal cage walls where every tool used in the plant was stored. The cage man moved fast, checking in and logging each nailer, hammer, pry bar, and screw gun as they were passed through the slot in the cage to him, each tool stamped with a *Crestline Homes* ID plate that bore a serial number. The nails and screws were doled out by the box at the start of each shift and charged against each man's rate. It behooved them to be as thrifty as possible with their fasteners, and as such, no one left their boxes lying around. Too many thieves in the lot that wouldn't hesitate to snatch up someone's nails if they forgot to hide them away in their locker at lunch. When you worked on rate, time was money, but so were tools.

Jimmy grabbed his bag from his locker and headed for the break room. He sat by himself, though more guys filled in the seats around him, the few who actually brought their own food from home. The majority of guys, on the short side of 25, dropouts and tweakers with cash to burn in their pockets, headed up the highway to the row of fast food joints lining each side. That or they headed off to someplace quiet where they could shoot up, smoke, snort, drink, or whatever their preferred delivery method might be. Lot of guys needed to be high to keep up the pace and make rate. None of them realized that shit was slowing them down over time. Jimmy didn't care either way, unless it was the laborer assigned to him. Whatever, as long as the junkie kept up with him.

Lost in his thoughts, Jimmy didn't hear the conversation behind him at first. Didn't take long to realize they were talking about him, though. Their voices were low, but not that low.

"What's his name again?"

"Jimmy Paradise. I seen him fight at Brown's in Chicago a few years back."

"That place in Downers Grove?"

"No, that one on the southside, Blue Island."

"Ain't that Sweeney's?"

"No, shithead, Sweeney's is a fuckin' bar. That's where Keith picked up that chick who gave him the clap."

"Then I never went to Brown's I guess."

"You've been there. Like a year ago we went."

"Was he any good?"

"Shit yeah, he was. Quick as a motherfucker. Light you up with the combination, Roy Jones Jr. style. Used to be his signature, they called it 'Two Tickets to Paradise'. The old one-two. Once he got inside a dude and worked the combo, it was over."

"Meldrick Taylor was faster than Jones."

"Now I know you're crazy. You smoke something before you came in here?"

"Hector Camacho."

"Yeah, you smoked some something, alright."

Another voice, older sounding, mouth full of food, piped up. "Sugar Ray Leonard."

The other two fell silent, apparently agreeing with this assessment.

The first guy eventually said, "He's so good, the fuck's he doin' here then?"

That was enough for Jimmy. He tossed his sandwich back in his bag and stood, walked from the room without so much as a glance at the table behind him. Breezed out the door, but stopped outside in the hall and listened. They kept at it.

"I heard he crossed some big shot, or some wannabe big shot in any case. The guy fucked his hand up. You see his right hand?"

"Yeah, fingers all kind of curled in and lumpy and shit. Like a retard's hand or something."

"Whoever he pissed off, dude took a hammer and pounded his hand into ground beef. That's the story told to me anyway."

Jimmy headed outside, couldn't stand to hear them talk. Heat of the day cranking up, blistering sun overhead. A new film of sweat washed over him, added to what already soaked into his clothes. Humid and sweltering, temperature in the 90s. No AC inside the plant. Lots of fans but all they did was shove the heat around. He walked across the road to the gas station on the other side, bought two Gatorades and a pack of cigarettes. Felt instantly guilty about the smokes but lit one up anyway. Annie would bitch him out, but only because if she couldn't have any, he shouldn't either.

Jimmy stood under an awning, out of the sun, drained one of the Gatorades, and just finished a second smoke when the buzzer sounded. He flicked the butt away and joined the herd mulling toward the tool cage, sweat running out of him like an open tap.

When the buzzer finally went off again at four o'clock, Jimmy was drenched and exhausted. The others grab-assed around the time clock, chatted at their lockers. Jimmy locked up his leftover nails and headed for his truck as fast as he could without running. He jammed his key into the lock and opened the door. Nearly hit the guy standing behind him with it. One of the talkers from the break room. Two more shuffling next to him.

"Hey," the guy said. "Jimmy, right?"

For an instant, Jimmy saw it going down, envisioned a left cross into the mouthy bastard's nose. One quick shot, mash his nose across his face. The others see all that blood and screaming and they back up fast. Jimmy needed a second to hold back, a deep breath.

"Yeah?"

"I thought that was you. I seen you fight before." The guy stuck his hand out. "I'm Vic, over in framing. These two assholes are Randy and Bobby."

One of the assholes took a half step forward and said, "My name's Andy, not Randy. Vic the dick thinks he a comedian."

"What's up, guys?"

"We was heading to Sara's for a beer," Vic said. "Wanted to know if you wanted to come down, hang with some of the guys."

Jimmy sighed. He was too damn hot and tired for this shit. "Not today fellas, OK?"

"Come on, man, you don't drink beer?"

"How much did you lose?"

Vic looked at his boys, laughed a little and said, "What's that?"

Jimmy closed his truck door, squared up in front of Vic. Set his feet, shoulder-length apart, offset just a bit. Ready to go. "When you saw me fight. You took one look at me, thought it was in the bag, placed your bet, and now you think I owe you something because I won and you lost."

Jimmy set his shoulders back and watched Vic's recognition of just how broad he really was. Bigger than he looked. Bigger guy than Vic was willing to tangle with, but now it was too late. Jimmy saw the look in his eyes, the realization that he just walked into a situation he suddenly wished he was no longer a part of. Vic laughed again, looked over his shoulder at his boys again, both of them shrinking back a step.

"I didn't. I never bet on your fight."

"No?"

Licked his lips, real nervous now. "No. I already lost all my money. Put it on the Polack in the welterweight bout right before yours. Asshole got knocked out in the second round."

Jimmy watched him for a second. Vic licked his lips again and Jimmy saw the guy was shaky. He was scared. Not at all the reaction he expected. Jimmy eased his shoulders down, relaxed and nodded. Tried to smile, set the guy at ease.

"Sorry, man. Sometimes guys come at me. Like I personally took their money."

Vic finally understood and looked back at Randy Andy and Bob. Seemed to understand what the three of them looked like, walking up on Jimmy together like that. "Oh shit. No, my fault, dude. Fuck, we was just coming to invite you to have a beer with us."

Jimmy opened his door again, a contrite smile on his face. "Thanks guys, I appreciate it, but I'm beat. Gonna head home now."

"OK, sure." Vic bobbed his head, filling with adrenaline and more nervous now that he saw how close he'd come to going toe-to-toe with a middleweight. "Maybe next time, OK? I'm buying."

"Sure thing, thanks."

Jimmy got in, started the truck, pulled out of the parking lot. Watched Vic and the boys in the rearview mirror, still standing there trying to comprehend what they almost got themselves into. He shook his head, swallowed the anxiety eating his gut. Felt bad for the way he jumped on those guys.

He lit up a cigarette and felt bad about that, too, but he smoked it anyway.

He woke up on the couch when Annie's key hit the lock. He hadn't meant to fall asleep in his filthy, sweat-damp work clothes, but it was that kind of day. He saw the reproach in her eyes when she walked in and got a look at him.

"Hey baby, how was your day?"

She sighed, dropped her purse and keys on the tiny table where they shared their meals, pulled off her coffee-and-whipped-cream-stained smock and tossed that on the back of a chair. Dropped into that chair and leaned back and sighed again.

"That bad, huh?"

"Some guy screamed at me for giving him a decaf."

"That's hardly worth screaming at someone over."

"Especially when it was the coffee his wife ordered for him while he was in the bathroom."

"Sounds like he needed that decaf."

"I gotta get out of that rest area. That toll road makes people insane. Like they're walking into Thunderdome when they come in."

"Just a little longer, till I get my next increase, then you won't have to do it anymore."

She smiled at him, meek, exhausted. She looked how he felt. Then she sat up, her nose to the air like a hound. Stared him down hard and he knew he was busted. Should have gotten a damn shower.

"You've been smoking, haven't you."

She wasn't asking him a question and it was impossible for him to lie to her, about anything, so he didn't even bother to try.

"Asshole, that's not fair."

"I know. Sorry. Long day."

Her scowl faded away. She looked him over and then she looked sad. He must be pathetic standing there in his dirty clothes. Bags under his eyes, shoulders slumped. Rubbing his right hand without even knowing he was doing it until her eyes fell on it. The crooked bones pulsed, sore and already getting arthritic. He was only twenty-six. Hated thinking about his age. About all the bills he had already, how many had already come due. Already been paid for, one way or another.

"I'll go get my shower now, unless you want to get in first."

Annie rubbed her belly, just barely a visible bump showing beneath her brown *Grinders* work shirt. "Go ahead. I think you need it more than me anyway. I just want to sit here and rest for a minute."

Jimmy walked over to her, squatted and placed his hand over hers, both of them rubbing her belly. "Everything OK?" Different question than 'how are you feeling.'

Annie shrugged, smiled, not quite as convincing. "Pretty good. At least I'm not throwing up anymore. Just standing all day is starting to kill my back and feet."

"I know. Another month and you're out of there. Promise."

She smiled, a real one this time, and gathered his salty, unshaven face in her hands and brought it up to hers and kissed him. He loved her so much it pressed on his lungs and burned behind his ribs. She had to endure so much just to stick by him. He could look in her eyes right then and see that she still thought he was worth it, but he wondered how long that would last. At what point does it stop being worth it? People get tired. They wear down. Becomes a case of diminishing returns.

Jimmy held her cheeks and kissed her back, deeply. Said, "I won't let that happen."

"Won't let what happen?"

He smiled and stood. "Nothing. Thinking out loud."

"Well, be careful, Punchy. You're liable to hurt something up there."

"I'm getting a quick shower now."

"OK, I'm sitting on my big, pregnant ass now."

"That's not a big ass. It's tiny."

"You weren't here this morning to watch me try to put my pants on."

Jimmy's quick shower took twenty minutes. Felt too good, cooled him off down to his bone marrow. Ten hours of working on the floor of a manufactured housing production plant would take the snap out of anyone's sails, no matter how in-shape they are. Not that Jimmy was in fighting shape any longer, but compared to Vic and the rest of the crew at Crestline, he was fit as a fiddle. He felt closer to normal after his shower, almost good even.

That mood lasted as long as it took to walk out of the bathroom and see Annie standing in the kitchen next to the front door. Arms folded tight under her breasts, which were definitely getting bigger with pregnancy if not her ass. Her face was inscrutable.

"What's wrong?"

She was pale, lips thin and bloodless. "You have a visitor."

Jimmy looked into the living room but saw no one. "Where?"

Annie nodded to the door. "Outside. I won't fucking let him in."

Whoever it was, it was bad. Jimmy got to the door, began to turn the knob, knew right then whom he would find out there.

Sully was slouched on the cheap Astroturf carpet that covered the walkway leading to their apartment, last on the second floor, end of the building. He stood, wobbly, a hand against the neighboring apartment's door. He got halfway up, half a smile breaking across his face when Jimmy dropped him with a left jab.

Sully lay on the floor, dazed. Annie creeped to the door and looked around Jimmy. Smacked his arm. "Dammit, Jimmy, why'd you hit him?"

"He's alright. I barely touched him."

Sully sat up a bit more, reflexively rubbing the red blotch on the side of his jaw, probably thanking God in his head that it wasn't broken. "It's fine, Annie. He took it easy on me. I deserve a lot more than that."

He did and knew it and Jimmy didn't bother reminding him. Sully knew that Jimmy should beat his ass to death, his face to wood pulp, but yet here he was, turning up on Jimmy's doorstep with a smile on his face. Like they were old friends needed catching up. Slowly, one finger at a time, Jimmy unlocked his fists. His right hand only opened halfway, ached like hell.

Sully got to his feet and Jimmy saw what little was left of him. Never was a thick kid by any stretch, but Sully was positively sickly now. Jimmy couldn't help himself, winced at his old friend. Wished he could take that punch back. He said, "Goddamn, Sully, what the hell?"

Sully looked down at his feet. Despite the heat, he wore long sleeves and still looked cold. His whole body trembled. "I look pretty bad, huh?"

"Yeah, you do."

"Well, I guess it *is* pretty bad." He looked up, eyes wide and wet. "It's ALS."

Jimmy pushed the door open for him, stood aside. Sully stayed where he was, watched Annie. She stood her ground, arms still tucked tightly around her chest. She scanned him up and down and looked at Jimmy. He tilted his head at her, said with his eyes, 'Just for a minute and then he's gone.' Annie shook her head and walked back into the apartment. They waited until they heard the door to the bedroom close. Jimmy said to Sully, "Come in."

"I didn't come here to rile up your old lady."

"It's alright, she's just tired."

"Liar."

Jimmy smiled, quick and then it was gone. "You thirsty? Or hungry?"

"Jimmy, man, you're my like my brother. More of a family to me than my real brother ever was. You know that, right?"

Jimmy did and nodded. "Come on."

Sully dropped his shoulders and his head and shuffled in. Jimmy stood in the open door for a second, watched the cars streaming by out on the road just beyond the trees that lined the apartment complex property. Then he shut the door.

Sully sat on the couch, looked around at the place. "Looks real nice," he said.

"Thanks." Jimmy sat in a battered recliner they picked up out by a dumpster when they moved in. "What are you doing here, Sully?"

He rubbed his skeletal hands together and stared at the carpet. His whole body shook with tremors. "I'm dying," he said to the floor.

"Soon?"

Sully shrugged, held his hands up. They bobbed in the air. His head wobbled like an old man's. "Maybe. Yeah, soon."

"Sorry for hitting you."

"Don't apologize. I need to do that."

Jimmy waited for him to do that. He didn't hold his breath, though.

"Jimmy, I fucked you over, man. I'm not even going to sit here and try to blame the drugs or say it was Sonny's fault. It's totally on me. I left you hung out to dry. Man, I know my word doesn't mean shit, but you have to believe me when I say that I'm truly sorry."

Sully's eyes fell back to the floor, but Jimmy was impressed he managed to hold his gaze all the way through that. Knew how hard it must have been for him. Jimmy got up and went to the fridge, pulled out two beers, popped the caps off, and handed one to Sully. He took it and pulled a pill bottle from the pocket of his jacket. Jimmy watched him and Sully held the bottle up.

"Don't worry, it's not street," he said. He washed the pills down with a long drink from his beer. "It's just diazapem. Supposed to help with the tremors." His hand still shook when he put the pill bottle back in his pocket. He laughed and said, "Not that they do much."

"So, what's the story? You have to take like chemo or have a surgery or something?"

Sully shook his head. "No cure for this. Just wait for it to get worse, until I'm a quivering bowl of jello and the lights upstairs go out."

Jimmy cracked a smile, couldn't help himself. "You still a Yankees fan?"

Sully grinned back and said, "Hell no. Fuck Lou Gehrig."

They laughed quietly. Not too loud, though, so Annie wouldn't think they were partying out there. Sully looked down the hall at the closed door and said, "She going to make you sleep on the couch for letting me in?"

"Nah, she'll be alright. She's just tired."

"She pregnant?"

"Yeah. About thirteen weeks now."

"Aw man, congratulations. That's awesome."

"Thanks."

Sully toasted him with his beer bottle and they drank in silence for a bit until Jimmy set his beer on the battered coffee table between them. "What are you doing here, Sully? I know you didn't just come to tell me you were sick."

"You know me, don't you?"

"You never come around unless you need something."

"Guilty." Sully sat back and shoved his hands in his jacket pocket. Pretended like he was fiddling with the pill bottle, but Jimmy could see him quivering, his head wobbly. "JP, I need a favor."

Jimmy said nothing, just waited to hear the spiel.

"I'm on my way to see Mom. Haven't seen her since I left Chicago. I know I shouldn't go back there, but what the fuck. I'm dying anyway, so what do I care if Sonny or anyone else catches up with me?"

Jimmy stared a hole through Sully, searching for the bullshit he knew was there.

"I'm out of money. Only had enough for a bus ticket to LaPorte. I want to see my mother one more time. Then what happens after that won't matter."

There it was. Jimmy said, "I don't have any money to give you, Sully. You see how we're living here."

"I know, and that's not what I'm asking for. I wouldn't do that to you considering what I owe you. All I'm asking is for a ride to Chicago. Mom's at Sacred Heart these days. Take about an hour to get there is all. You'll be back home in two, maybe three depending on traffic. All you have to do is drive me there and drop me."

"And then what will you do?"

"There's more folks to see besides Mom. I know a couple couches I can crash on."

"More people to see." Jimmy shook his head. Looked up at the ceiling. "You know what you're asking me here, right?"

"I know, and like I said, you just drop me off and head back home, that's it. Don't even have to get out of the car."

"It's that simple, huh?"

"That simple."

"Sully, nothing's that simple with you."

Sully didn't respond. Nothing he could say to that.

"You might be sick, and you might be dying, but you don't have any favors left. You used those up a long time ago."

Sully looked at the door. Saw it was time to leave. Got up slow and said, "Thanks for the beer, man."

He got to the door and had a hand on the knob when Jimmy said, "Hang on."

Sully stood facing the door. His whole body shook.

"Give me a minute to talk to Annie, OK?"

Sully turned around. Tears in his eyes. "Yeah, OK. Thank you."

Jimmy got up and headed for the bedroom. Tapped on the door and went in. Annie was on the bed, looking out the window.

"Are you taking him?" she said.

"You heard all that?"

She nodded.

"I don't know what I'm doing yet. Wanted to get your opinion first."

"Just the fact that you haven't said no yet tells me you've made up your mind already. You just don't realize it."

"I haven't made my mind up yet."

She looked at him. Almost rolled her eyes but didn't. "He wants you to take him back to Chicago."

"He's dying. He wants to see his mother."

"Jimmy, I love you, but you're a fool. You're too trusting and assholes like Anthony Sullivan pick you out of a crowd. They prey on you because they can."

Every word true, Jimmy knew it. But it didn't change his mind, which he realized was in fact already made up. Which meant she was right, again. He didn't have the words to speak further. Didn't want to be pissed at her for being right. Just sat and stared out the window with her.

Annie finally turned to him and said, tears standing in her eyes, "Just get it over with, but goddammit, Jimmy, this is it for that asshole. You make him *know* that. Even if you have to break your other hand on his fucking face for him to get it through his head."

"Don't worry, he'll know."

"I fucking mean it, Jimmy." Her voice cracked and Jimmy knew she would lose it once they left. Cry herself to sleep tonight. He hated to do it to her, but this had to be done.

"You finish this with him."

"I will. And then I can put Chicago behind me forever."

Jimmy smiled at his wife, promised this to her with his eyes. Kissed her forehead, got up and shut the door behind him and didn't believe a word of what he said.

They pulled away from the apartment complex, headed down the two-lane county road. Stopped at the Mobil station along the way and filled up the truck's tank. Headed back out toward U.S. 6.

Not a word between them until Sully said, "You taking 94 in?"

"Yeah, why?"

"Man, it's gonna be a parking lot this close to rush hour."

Jimmy cut a glance across the bucket seat and said, "The only money I had with me just went into the gas tank. That was supposed to last me until Friday. Unless you have cash to pay for the Skyway, we're taking 94."

"Fuck that, I ain't wasting money on the toll road."

"OK then."

"I got enough left for a burger, though."

"Congratulations."

"Come on, man, I'm starving. We can stop and grab a bite, let the traffic clear out a bit. And I bet you haven't had dinner yet, either. Have you?"

The idea of a burger started a revolt in Jimmy's guts. Somewhere under his seat was his leftover lunch from the afternoon, a half-eaten turkey sandwich that had spent the last six hours cooking inside the truck.

"You're buying," he said.

"Shit yeah, I'm buying."

"McDonalds is right near the ramp for 94."

"Fuckin' McDonalds? Hell no." Sully pointed to the left side of the road at Sara's Place, a squat, squalid shack with a blinking sign that only half worked, about a quarter mile off. "What about this place coming up?"

"So are you hungry or thirsty?"

"I can't hardly eat anything anymore. All that fucking medication I'm on makes me sick as a dog. My doctor has me on a liquid diet."

Sully grinned at him and Jimmy shook his head, beating down the urge to smile back. Slick little bastard. Jimmy pulled into the parking lot and they shuffled into Sara's, Jimmy feeling sick with unease at how fast they fell back into their old, familiar patter. Like two years and an ocean of hard living hadn't separated them. He wished he would have listened to Annie. Wished that, but kept putting one foot in front of the other until they were sitting at a greasy table in the corner of the bar, giving their orders to the waitress. Cheeseburger and ice water for Jimmy, shot and a beer for Sully. Old fucking times.

"You think she digs the sick look?"

"What?"

Sully pointed at the waitress as she walked back to the kitchen. "Chick like her, you think she'd dig the whole Make a Wish vibe I got going? 'Hey baby, I got three months to live and I wanna spend them all with you.'"

"You're an asshole."

Sully shrugged. "Bet it would be worth a blowjob anyway. Maybe a quick handie in the bathroom."

Jimmy laughed in spite of himself.

"Hey, Jimmy fucking Paradise is in the house!"

Jimmy looked around for the voice, loud and drunk. Vic from the plant, stumbling his way over from the bar. His two buddies, Randy Andy and the other dude, whatever his name was Jimmy forgot, sitting hunched at the bar, watching over their shoulders. Not at all interested in coming near Jimmy.

"Hey JP, who's this asshole?"

"It's alright, just some guy from work. They've been in here boozing since we knocked off this afternoon."

"Oh, wonderful. Friends in low places, huh?"

Jimmy rolled his eyes at Sully, turned to Vic. "Hey Vic, how's it going?"

"Thought you was tired. Didn't expect to see you in here."

"Yeah, I took a power nap when I got home."

Vic laughed, a little too earnestly. Still shaken from this afternoon. He pulled out the remaining empty chair at the table and dropped into it.

"Yeah, sure buddy, have a seat," Sully said, not bothering to hide his annoyance.

"Thanks, man." To Jimmy he said, "Hey, whatever you're getting, it's on me, OK?"

"No, Vic, that's alright. My good friend Sully here is buying."

"Fuck you, let the man talk." Sully to Vic: "You were saying, something about the tab?"

Vic, in a fog of drunken confusion, "Yeah, these are on me. I mean it. I feel bad about this afternoon, the way we kind of jumped on you there."

Sully's eyebrows arched. "What's this? Trouble in River City?"

"It was nothing. Just a misunderstanding."

Jimmy began to tell Sully that he wasn't going to talk about it, but he stopped. Watched his old friend, his elbows on the table, eager to hear a tale of near-violence. Jimmy decided to tell one.

He turned to Vic and said, "Where are my manners? Sully, this is Vic from Crestline Homes. He's a framer, one of the best, too."

Vic nodded, grinned like a chick at the flattery. Sully saluted him, but the sarcasm went over Vic's inebriated head.

"Vic, this here is Andrew Sullivan. Sully and I have known each other since we met in fourth grade at St. Stanislaus. That's on the south side."

Vic said, "Yeah? South side of Chicago?"

Sully rolled his eyes. "No, Magellan, the south side of Calcutta."

Vic nodded, just missed grasping the insult.

To Sully, Jimmy said, "Vic and his buddies recognized me from my boxing days. He came up to say hello, but I mistook his gesture and thought perhaps they had once wagered against me and came out on the wrong side, and therefore wanted to recoup their losses."

"Like that asshole out in Joliet?"

"Yeah, or the four guys over in Gary."

"Fucking Gary. I told you to stay the hell out of that town."

"Indeed, you did. I should have listened."

Vic looked back and forth, eyes wide. Sully said, "It turned out alright, JP broke the first guy's nose with a left jab, then broke his jaw with a right hook. The other three probably never ran faster in their lives."

Vic laughed, smacked the table, swilled beer.

"Yeah, we got a million stories," Jimmy said. Sully's face dropped. Saw where this was headed. Sat back in his chair as the waitress set their drinks in front of them.

"Burger's coming right up, hon."

"Thanks."

Vic said to the waitress, "Hey Sis, they're on my tab, and I'll take another one, too."

Sis rolled her eyes at Vic, walked away. Sully drank his beer and stared at some far off void beyond the tacky table in front of him. Vic watched Jimmy, waiting for him to go on, tell another tale of ass kicking.

"We definitely have a million stories together." Jimmy looked away from Sully, focused on Vic. Held up his right hand, fingers curled toward the palm in a loose half-fist. "I ever tell you about how I got this?"

Vic's smiled dropped away. He shook his head. Said, "Huh-uh," like he really didn't want to hear it, either.

"You'll like this one." Jimmy cracked his neck and sat up straight, prepared to dive into the tale. Ready to spin a yarn.

"OK, so this was a couple years back. My good pal Sully here was also my manager back in those days. He was the guy who I entrusted with finding fights for me, get me lined up with promoters and venues and advance my career that maybe one day I could challenge for a title. That's the big dream, you know? I fought middleweight, even though I was always on the lighter end of that class. I had to work hard to keep my weight up, and I was almost always the lighter fighter. I think that's why most people bet against me in the beginning, when I first got going. I guess I didn't cut a very intimidating figure back then.

"I fought a lot early on, mainly because I could, I was maybe a little impatient, and because Sully kept getting me fights. Had to climb those rankings and work hard to get a shot, right? Maybe we moved a little too fast, took some fights we shouldn't have, or at least waited longer between fights to rest up, refocus and whatnot. My trainer, my coach, everybody saying slow down, but me and Sully saying, 'No, let's go. Get paid, move on.' Promoters liked us because we helped fill out a card if they were in a tight spot. I lost a few early in my career that I should have won. But I was also known as a good fighter, tough to knock out, always a good battle. I had a good skill set, quick with the punches. You really had to be on your toes to get into me, which made a good barometer for other guys. If you can't get Jimmy Paradise, maybe you weren't good enough for the next level. So, instead of being the guy on the rise, I sort of became the guy that the real guys on the rise wanted to fight. A good resume builder, right? I faced a bunch of really good fighters, and I managed to win more than I lost."

Vic's buddies strolled up, drawn in by the story. Chatter in the bar lighter as others listened in.

"So along comes this kid, Alcides Ochoa." A few heads nodded, a familiar name. No doubt some of these guys already heard a version of this, but not the one Jimmy was telling.

"Ochoa's undefeated, something like fifteen and oh, real hot commodity, and his people are just itching for that title shot. Lot of people in his corner, backers want to see him go far, think he's got the tools and the talent to win the belt right now. But they say he needs one more fight. Somebody good, a name that makes people sit up and take notice. Somebody like a Jimmy Two Tickets to Paradise. They say a win over Jimmy Paradise will make Ochoa the top contender for the WBC crown, and once they take that first one, the title shots will line up one after the next. That's what they think of Ochoa, that he'll hold all the belts. The next undisputed middleweight champ. The next Hagler or Ray Robinson."

Couple of disbelieving chuckles from the crowd, dozens of heads turned to Jimmy now, hanging on every word.

"No, really, they thought he was that good. Had that kind of potential. Obviously, we know now that Alcides Ochoa was not the next Sugar Ray Robinson, but when a young guy's coming up like that, knocking out suckers left and right and has that certain something, that combination of power and speed and flair, that's when a whole lot of people start seeing dollar signs. Tends to cloud their judgment. They want to get in on a kid like that early and ride him on the way up. There was a lot of money backing Ochoa and at that point, they wanted one thing: a fight that would cement a title shot, but only if it was a sure thing. He had to win."

Jimmy let the crowd digest that a minute while he sipped his ice water. Several sets of eyes fell on Sully, who continued to stare at the table, pretending not to listen, face still as stone. Jimmy watched him for a moment, noticed that the tremors, gone for a second, were back. He considered stopping, but he was past that point. This had to be told. He had to get it out. The first and last time for this story.

"Enter Sonny Porter," Jimmy continued. "Kind of a small-timey promoter, thought he was bigger than he really was. Greasy bastard that people had trouble trusting, and for good reason. Kind of like Ochoa, he needed something to boost his cred among the circles he ran in. Getting the Ochoa fight lined up was his ticket to bigger and better things. If he could deliver a sure thing with a credible opponent, he would be on the ins with a lot of folks. At the time, I didn't know about any of this. Why would I, right? I'm a fighter, I fight. When I don't fight, I train. Workout, run, spar. I leave all that other shit to my manager to handle. And that's what he did.

"Sully lined up the fight with Porter and Ochoa's people, was going to be on Pay-Per-View and everything. And he made it happen by making a promise. In round five, I go down, and Ochoa goes on to secure his title shot. For that, we get an extra twenty grand from one of Ochoa's 'sponsors.'" Jimmy made air quotes with his fingers. All eyes were on Sully now and the bar was quiet. He remained stone-faced, and to his credit, didn't sweat.

"But I never knew any of this, not until the night of the fight. The whole time, I think I'm training for the biggest fight of my life. Probably the one that sets my career back on track if I win. Imagine what beating Ochoa would do for me. Score a win on TV, lots of eyes watching to see if this Ochoa kid is the real deal, instead see me come out and whip his ass? That's what was in my head.

"So fast forward. It's fight night. Arena is packed, cameras and reporters and all kinds of excitement. The place was electric. I'm in my dressing room, waiting for the start, pumping myself up." Jimmy punctuated the feeling, put his hands up by his face, shadow punched across the table, his hands a blur. A ripple of appreciation went through the crowd.

"I'm loose, I'm confident that I'll knock this kid flat on his ass, I'm ready to go. Five minutes before the fight, who walks in but Sonny Porter. One of his goons trailing behind him. Sully cuts him off, but he wants to talk to me. Wants to be absolutely sure that this goes down the way it was designed. Lot riding on this outcome, for a lot of people. Sonny's let a few choice folks in on the fix, got them to plunk down some serious cash. I think Ochoa was laying four hundred points, so if they wanted a payoff on that sure thing, they had to pony up big time. He wants to make sure I understand this."

Jimmy, everyone else, watching Sully. A statue. Jimmy wondered if he was even breathing anymore.

"That's when I learned of the deal Sully cut for me. Guaranteed Sonny Porter and Ochoa's corner that I would go down in the fifth. Drop my guard, eat a big right, stay down for the count. It was going to be a really good win for Alcides Ochoa, the next Sugar Ray Robinson."

A guy sitting behind Sully leaned over and said in his ear, "You're a real piece of shit, huh pal?"

"Hold on," Jimmy said. "It gets better. Sonny leaves, and I'm coming out of my skin. I'm ready to tear my good friend here a brand new asshole. How can he do this to me? How can he expect me to throw this fight? He tells me it's just one fight. That I've lost before, and to worse fighters than Ochoa. It won't hurt my career. And besides, we needed the money."

Jimmy shook his head at Sully, talked directly to him. "I didn't need the money, Sully. You needed it. You were the one in trouble. Desperate to get the sharks off your back. You didn't do it for me. You did it for you. And where did all that cash you walked away with go, huh? Flushed it all away, didn't you? Shot it all up your arm."

Silence in the bar for a beat, then Vic leaned over and said, "But you won that fight. How did he get paid if you didn't go through with the fix?"

Jimmy cracked a smile that contained no humor. "That's the best part. Old Sully here, he's a smart kid. Smarter than he looks by a long shot. He had it all planned out. Knew exactly what would happen. Hell, he even invited Sonny to come back to the locker room before the fight, just so it would play out this way. I find out about the fix, he plays dumb about why he did it, I go out there full of piss and vinegar and righteous indignation and proceed to put an ass-whipping on Alcides Ochoa the likes of which he has yet to recover from. Ref should have stopped it in the first round, but he let it go on. I dropped Ochoa in the second with the first combination I put on him. The place goes apeshit. I go back to the dressing room after the ringside interviews, but Sully's not there. He's not, but Sonny Porter is. Sully was off collecting on the bet he put down. Yeah, he knew exactly what I was going to do. Played me like a fiddle, man. He took the underdog in that fight, and made out like a bandit. What'd you win again? Something like fifty K?"

Sully shrugged, shrank in his chair a bit.

"It's all gone now, of course. Probably has been for a while too. He took off to, what was it, Memphis? I think it was Memphis, by way of St. Louis. Whatever it was, Sully was gone. And I was left to explain what happened to Sonny Porter."

Jimmy held up his right hand for the bar to see. "This is what Sonny thought of my explanation."

Sis the waitress placed Jimmy's burger in front of him and pointed at Sully. "You're a piece of fucking shit," she said.

Vic said to Sully, "How the hell could you do something like that to a person you called a friend?" Turned to Jimmy and said, "What they hit you with? I heard it was a drywall hammer."

Jimmy shook his head, said around a mouthful of grease and cheese, "Nope, sledgehammer."

The crowd winced in unison. More catcalls reigned down on Sully. He looked around, nervous and waiting for someone to come at him. Jimmy saw that it could turn ugly at any moment, but he waited a little longer, savored the scene. It was good to see Sully squirm. Lord knew the little shithead deserved more. Even a year ago, if they had been sitting in that bar as they were then, Jimmy would have simply stood up and strolled out, got in his truck and gone home. Left Sully to deal with the mob on his own.

He deserved it. But Jimmy wasn't going to let it happen. Before the drunks got too close and touched something off, he stood and said in a loud, hard voice, "But we're not here to dwell on the past. I used to work out my grievances with my fists, but I'm not a fighter anymore. Life is too short for that nonsense." He looked down at Sully, at his quaking hands, twitching head. Tremors coming on full blast. "I see that now."

The crowd murmured at that a bit, but they eased up. Jimmy still knew it was time to go. He had his fun. The mob backed away as Sully and Jimmy headed for the door.

"You trying to get me killed?"

Jimmy hit the I-94 ramp and gunned the truck into the moderate traffic zipping along at 80 miles per hour. "That's funny, I've wanted to ask you that very question for a long time."

"I apologized, JP. You know I wasn't right in the head back then. If I could take back what I did to you, I would."

"But you can't, so there's no point in talking about it now."

Quiet for a minute, no more than that. Sully smiled and said, "You remember that fat kid from St. Stan's? Joey Bell? Used to bloody your nose for you until I came up behind him and kicked him in the nuts?"

Jimmy said nothing.

"The rumor was one of his testicles burst and the doctors told him he'd never have kids?" He laughed, waited for Jimmy to crack, laugh with him. It didn't happen.

"I'm done with reminiscing," Jimmy said, voice quivering.

If Sully said another word, Jimmy didn't think he'd be able to keep from busting his lip. Anger and empathy fought for control, but neither won out. The sight of his old friend, sickly and dying, wasn't enough to tamp down the entrenched rage he'd nurtured for two years. Not something he could simply brush aside, no matter how pathetic Sully looked. Sully must have sensed it, too. He looked out the window and said nothing for several miles. Jimmy welcomed the quiet and drove.

It was completely dark outside when they neared the state line. Jimmy could see Sully shaking out of the corner of his eye, bouncing to a silent beat. A road sign informed them of places to stop and eat or get gas and Sully perked up in his seat.

"Hey, we need to make a pit stop."

"I'm not stopping until we get to Sacred Heart. And even then I'm only going to slow down enough for you to jump out."

"That's what you want to do, that's cool, but your seat's gonna be covered in piss in about ten seconds. These meds fuck up my bladder control. Can't hold it much longer."

The exit was coming up fast. At the last second, Jimmy, swerved across two lanes and took it. He pulled into a Speedway station and parked on the side of the building.

"You have five minutes," he said. "If it takes you six to piss, you're walking the rest of the way."

"Alright, I get it."

Sully got out and shuffled into the station. Jimmy

drummed his fingers on the steering wheel and watched the clock. Green digital minutes ticked by. At five minutes, and no sight of Sully, he put the truck in reverse. And sat there, his foot mashing the brake pedal. He should just leave, he knew it. Instead, he shut the truck off and went inside.

A tremendous fat woman sat behind the counter, barely lifted her eyes at him before returning them to the book in her hands. Jimmy headed to the back, steamed toward the two doors marked GUYS and GALS and put all his weight behind the kick. The GUYS door flew open, smashed against wall. Sully's head jerked up, shocked and scared. Like he was expecting a moment like this for a long time, only the guy on the other side of the door would be carrying a gun.

Jimmy looked down at Sully's arm. The sleeve of his jacket pushed up to his shoulder. Belt tied off above the elbow. Empty needle dangling from Sully's bone-skinny, scabbed up arm. Jimmy shook his head and walked away without a word.

"Fuck, JP, hang on, man."

Sully scrambled to collect his things, chase after Jimmy, who was already pushing out the door. The fat clerk behind the counter shouted after him, "Hey, you broke that door. Hey, come back here!"

Jimmy gunned the truck and nearly ran Sully down as he scrambled out in front of the grill. Jimmy held the brake down with his left foot and gunned the gas with his right. Sully screamed and jumped back, but he didn't move out of the way.

"Dammit, JP, let me in the truck!" Jimmy didn't respond and Sully said, "Man, give me a break with this self-righteous crap. You don't know what I go through with this shit. The only quality of life I got left is what I get outta that needle." Eyes shining, near tears. He said, "You don't know fucking shit, man."

"Don't move," Jimmy said out the window. "It'll be quicker if I hit you square on."

Sully dropped his hands to his sides and stood up straight. The fear fell away from his face. "Alright, go ahead," he said. "You want to do this, then do it. I ain't afraid to die. I'm already fucking dead, JP. You might as well finish me off if it makes you feel better."

Jimmy gunned the engine again, but Sully didn't flinch. They remained that way for several moments until Jimmy relented and geared the truck into park. Sully, white as paper in the glare of the headlights, shuffled forward, opened the passenger door. Got in and leaned his head against the window. Said nothing more.

Jimmy didn't drive off right away. Waited until his breathing normalized. Told Sully, "I better never see you again after tonight. If you turn up again, I won't hold back."

Sully shoved his hands into his pockets and turned his face to the window.

THIS EVENING

The cellphone in his breast pocket buzzed against his nipple. He pulled it out, took a deep breath, exhaled slowly.

"Nichols."

"Detective, we got a call into the precinct you might be interested in."

"Why's that?"

"Some guy over in Indiana, says he might have information about one of your burn victims."

"What kind of information?"

"Like he might have seen the guy the night of."

"I'll be there in twenty."

He clicked the phone off and tossed it onto passenger seat. From the glove box, he pulled out a small handheld black light. The bulb glowed blue and he moved it up and down his pants, searching for any stray splatters. Next he did his shirt and then the car door and the floor beneath his feet. Satisfied he hadn't brought any of the alderman with him, he started the Caprice and edged away from the curb.

He was parked three blocks away from the alderman's apartment building, a stately brownstone on a shady street where the neighbors knew to keep their blinds drawn and their mouths shut. Nichols still took no chances. Sims' nephew was a popular figure in his ward. The shit would hit the fan big time once they found his body.

Nichols drove just under the speed limit. He turned down a poorly-lit alley about five blocks away and chucked the little .25 pistol out the passenger window, into an open dumpster out back of a closed barbeque joint. The alderman's wallet, emptied of its cash, went out next and splashed in a puddle. When they found the gun and ran the ballistics, the name Curtis Telfair would ping back. Poor Curtis wouldn't tell them much, though, as he'd been buried in a pauper's grave some ten months now, gunned down in a crack house, probably by the shot-gunned Haitian kid Nichols took the gun off outside the liquor store. The file on Telfair would reveal a deal gone bad between junkies. No suspect ever arrested, no justice for poor Curtis Telfair. Another statistic in a city full of them.

Nichols wheeled the Caprice into the empty parking lot of a bakery with wood over the windows. He pulled behind the building and shut the car off. He went to the trunk, pulled out a folder, plastic bucket, and a bottle of lighter fluid. He set the bucket on the cracked pavement, dropped the folder into it, reached in his pocket and produced a flashdrive, which also landed in the bucket. Sprayed lighter fluid over everything, lit a match, dropped it and the whole book of matches inside.

Once the bucket began to melt and collapse, Nichols tossed the lighter fluid back into the trunk. He removed the latex gloves he was wearing and tossed them into the fire, then got back in the car and drove away.

PART III:
SETTLING UP

They were in Chicago 30 minutes later. Jimmy followed 94 north, merged onto the Dan Ryan, which teemed with summer traffic even at ten o'clock.

"I need you to get off at 76th."

"Why would I get off at 76th? Sacred Heart is north of Midway. Be quicker if I cut over to the Stevenson."

"Because I don't want you to drop me at Sacred Heart."

Jimmy looked across the bench seat. "What is *this* shit now? You want me to swing by your dealer? You can go fuck yourself, man."

"No, it's not like that. I know a guy has a body shop off of 76th. He's holding onto something and I need to get it."

"No fucking way. I'm dropping your ass at the nearest street corner. I'm done with this bullshit."

"It's not something for me. It's something that belongs to you."

"Yeah, like what?"

"Twenty thousand dollars."

"The hell you say."

The exit for 76th came up and Jimmy hesitated a moment, but took it.

"Where the hell would you get twenty thousand? And what makes you think I want your fucking money, anyway?"

Sully closed his eyes and laid his head against the window again. "Because now you need it."

"I'm not getting caught up in another one of your fucked up schemes, Sully. It's not happening."

"It's not a scheme. The money's already there. My guy is waiting for me. All we have to do is walk in, collect it, and you're heading back home. And then you and I are square."

Jimmy scoffed. "So you think twenty thousand is enough to make up for my hand? My fucking career?"

Sully shook his head. "No, but that's the best I can do."

"Where'd the money come from?"

Silence. Sully watched the side streets roll past.

"Either tell me or I stop right here."

"Alright. The truth is, my mom's not at Sacred Heart."

"Is that right? Where is she then?"

"She's dead."

Jimmy's turn to clam up. He wondered if it was true or just more bullshit from a professional bullshit artist. "When?"

"About three months ago."

Traffic got heavy and they crawled along at five miles per hour. People all over the streets. Shouting, laughing, arguing. Summer in Chicago made folks crazy with the heat, still in the 80s and humid. Jimmy's shirt stuck to his chest, wet down the back. Sully sat with his window still up, jacket zipped to the top, arms jammed in his pockets. He could have been a cadaver sitting there, if not for the tremors.

"You didn't go to her funeral, did you?"

Sully shook his head.

"You still didn't tell me where the money came from."

"Her estate. My big inheritance, the money left over from the sale of her house, less taxes and what the nursing home took to cover her bill."

"And how much was left?"

"About twenty-six thousand."

"You have twenty-six thousand dollars waiting for you in a body shop on the south side, and you're just going to hand over most of it to me."

"Yes." No further explanation.

"Sully, man, you're so full of shit. You think I'm going to believe this crap you're slinging at me?"

"You do what you want, I'm not making you do anything."

"Why a body shop? Late at night on a Friday in this part of town? Who is this guy of yours?"

"The guy is the lawyer in charge of Mom's estate. An old family friend. He's the one got Mom into Sacred Heart and he's the one who contacted me when she died. The only way I could get the money is if I came to pick it up from him in person. I explained to him my tenuous social status in this city and he suggested the body shop. It's his brother-in-law's joint. In and out fast, get the money and get the hell out of Chicago before anyone finds out I'm back. Hang a right at the next light."

Jimmy flipped on his directional, perfunctory, not even thinking about it. Poking holes in Sully's story until it looked like Swiss cheese. He knew there was no way any of this was true. Couldn't be, no matter how convincing Sully was, with his matter-of-fact attitude and vibrating muscles. Every bit of sense in Jimmy said to go no further.

He beat that voice of reason down, and hard. He thought of Annie and the baby and what twenty thousand dollars could mean for them. A house. New car that you didn't have to worry about getting started in the morning. Annie could quit that shit hole toll road rest stop coffee corral. Jimmy never was greedy when it came to himself, but when it came to Annie and their child…

"Where is this place already?"

Sully eyed him quickly and said, "Keep going, it's the second right up here. Narrow street, kind of looks like an alley."

They pulled up to it, Charlton Avenue. The street light at the corner was busted and the entire block was a corridor of black. Jimmy turned and crept along. They watched the crumbled store fronts and derelict homes pass, one empty lot after another, houses burned and razed, like dead teeth pulled from a rotting mouth. More sheets of plywood than glass in the windows of the remaining structures.

"It's on the right up here. See the awning hanging out over the sidewalk?"

"I don't see shit. Don't they believe in streetlights around here?"

"Dealers give the neighborhood kids twenty-two pistols to shoot them out. Soon as the city replaces the bulbs, they get broken the next day."

Nothing moved on either side of the street, but Jimmy had the distinct, eerie sensation of eyes on them, watching the two white boys in the rusty pickup truck tooling along through the hood.

"We're going to get fucking shot down here."

Sully pointed to the left side of the street. "There's a space, park right there."

"But I'm pointing the wrong way."

"Dude, I don't think you'll get a ticket over here."

They drove by the burned-out shell of a car and Jimmy pulled into the open space. "Yeah, I guess you're right."

He was nervous, possibly scared, but wouldn't admit that much, not even to himself. He turned off the truck and they sat in the dark watching the front door of the body shop until he couldn't stand it any longer.

"What the hell now, you going in or what?"

"Yeah, I'm just waiting a sec. I wanna see what's what out here."

"You don't think this lawyer's here or something?"

"Not that, I know the guy is here, but I'm not exactly comfortable just strolling around this hood with a bag full of money."

"Why didn't you just have it direct deposited into a bank account or something? Why the hell would this guy come out here with a sack of cash?"

Sully hesitated for just a second before saying, "Only way I'd accept the money. I don't have a bank account."

That was the point Jimmy finally knew the story was a total fabrication. Maybe not the existence of the money, though even that was dubious. Little Andrew Sullivan, his best bud from grade school, his one-time manager, a kid he'd known almost his whole life, was lying through his fucking teeth. Again. Like he always did. Jimmy squeezed the steering wheel, seethed and cursed up in his head at his stupidity.

"Turn off your dome light."

Jimmy would let him get out, wait for him to go inside the body shop, and just drive away. And if Sully showed his face on his doorstep again, then he would beat him to death and hide the body in a place no one would find it.

"Dude, I said turn off your dome light. I don't want it go on when I open the door."

Jimmy thumbed the button on the dash and Sully quietly popped the door open. He stepped out and scanned the street again, watching and listening. Held the handle up when he shut the door so it wouldn't make a noise. Looked up and down the street one more time and shuffled toward the body shop. He stopped and listened at the door, a metal job with vertical bars facing out and a piece of solid sheet metal on the inside in place of a screen. He pulled it open without a sound and stuck his head in. Jimmy heard him say something, just above a whisper, then he went inside and shut the door behind him.

Nothing moved on Charlton Avenue. Distant noise, echoes from the busier thoroughfares, drifted in through the truck's open driver-side window, but Charlton felt abandoned. Like anyone with sense knew to stay the hell away from this hood once the sun went down. Jimmy sat there and wished he had some sense.

Forces went to war inside him, battled to take control of his nervous system, work his arms and legs to put the truck in gear and drive away from there. The other faction locked him down and said, *Just wait for a minute.* Just to see. He had to know for certain there wasn't twenty thousand dollars about to walk out that door and drop into his lap. Despite already being convinced that would never happen, he still sat there. Watched the body shop and waited. Eyes flicked from the door to the digital clock in the truck's dash. One minute passed, then a second. He couldn't move. Could only sit there and try to rationalize what he was doing. He failed. Couldn't come up with a single angle that would convince him that he was making the smart move here. Not one.

And still he sat there, watched and waited, and finally the door opened and someone came out. Jimmy nearly reached over and popped the door open for Sully when he realized the form that stood under the awning was much taller and broader than his dying friend. Jimmy dropped down as low as he could without losing sight of the person across the street. The person stood and watched, head turning in the shadows one way, then the other. Scanned the street like Sully. Looking for whoever dropped him off, whoever was out here waiting for him to come back. Looking for Jimmy.

The figure moved out from under the awning, headed toward the truck, still on the opposite side of the street. Leaned over and looked in the cars parked there, crossed and started his way back up the other side. Jimmy thought about dropping down into the well beneath the steering column then quickly realized that he would only compound his stupidity. It was dark enough that you couldn't see into the cars until you were right on them, so he reached out and grabbed the door handle. When the guy was close enough, push the door open and catch the guy, maybe knock him off balance, slide across the bench seat, commence to beating his ass right there in the street.

But the guy stopped and just looked at the burned car. Looked at the boarded-up house in front of him, the vinyl siding on the front of the porch sagging and half-melted, probably from the blaze. The guy reached into his jacket, pulled something out, held his hands to his face. A weak orange light appeared in his cupped hands as he lit his cigarette and Jimmy saw who it was. Ricky's was a hard face to forget.

Ricky stood there and smoked a minute before turning back to the body shop. He opened the front door, looked around one last time, and headed back inside.

A thrumming ache started in Jimmy's clenched right hand, a tight, lumpy fist. If Ricky was here, that meant Sonny was, too. Sully was in there with both of them, and God knows who else. Jimmy had no idea what he would be walking into.

But he already had his mind made up what he would do. A few people inside that building owed him. They took his whole life. Jimmy decided he would go take some of it back.

He got out of the truck, careful not to slam the door. Quivering with rage that he had to hold back by biting his cheek until he tasted blood. He had no plan, probably would wind up getting himself killed right here. Didn't care. Something had always told him this was coming. Eventually, this had to happen. Nothing got solved with that sledgehammer. When he left Chicago, he couldn't get very far, and there was still a mess to fix. Now was the time.

Jimmy crouched next to the door and listened. Put his ear against the cool corrugated metal exterior wall. Low voices, not shouting or carrying on. The front of the building lacked windows of any kind. He thought about that, about going in completely blind, unarmed. He'd try the door first. Take a peek inside, see what he could see. If it looked bad, he was gone.

Jimmy pulled down on the door handle, painfully slow, afraid of a rusty screech from the battered metal. It moved fluidly, without a sound. He cracked it open just enough to allow a thin sliver of weak light through. He saw up the left side of the shop, a long tool bench made of cobbled together metal, crudely welded, covered with a smorgasbord of car parts and tools, piled into small mountains on top of the bench and underneath. Saw a squat, round Weber grill on the floor, tendrils of heat bending the air around it. Smelled the charcoal cooking inside.

He cracked the door wider, slow as he could manage, until the light grew stronger and he could make out the frame of an open doorway and glimpse the cheap wood paneling that covered the near wall of what looked like an office. The voices were louder, but still at normal speaking levels. Muted conversation that Jimmy still couldn't make out. He risked a look inside the shop, stuck his head through and glanced around the corner to the right. Nothing there but a pile of beat-up office furniture, stacks of pipes and sundry lengths of metal. Angle iron and the like. A pile accumulating for the scrap yard, probably. Jimmy slipped inside and pulled the door shut without a sound.

He crept toward the office, nearly stepped in a dark puddle of something, probably oil. He looked around on the bench top nearest to him for any kind of weapon. He picked up a pipe wrench that glistened in the low light from the office, the hook jaw slick with more oil. Jimmy sniffed it and realized it wasn't oil at all, probably not on the floor either. He held it in front and slipped along the wall until he was next to the office doorway. The closer he got, the stronger the smell of not only charcoal, but of something like burned hair, mixed with shit and piss. He tried not to gag.

From inside the office, Sully said, "He dropped me here and left."

Followed by Sonny Porter: "Is that right. I'm amazed he took you this far. Jimmy was always a loyal kid, to a fault when it came to your sorry ass."

Sully didn't respond. Jimmy heard a ripping sound but couldn't place it.

Sonny said, "You had to know there was no way you'd collect this money. Didn't you?"

More ripping. Sounded like a roll of tape unfurling.

"You couldn't go to any of the sports books because they've got your picture up on their walls. They all know you after the last time you pulled this. So you tried to use the lawyer. Sent him to Sims to place your bet and pick it up. What you didn't realize is that I knew all of this before the fight. I could have taken care of the lawyer whenever I wanted. That wasn't the best move, going with that guy. Know what he was doing when Ricky visited him? Packing a bag. He was on his way out the door with your money, which is now my money. Wanna see it?"

Sound of a zipper, a rustling noise. Sonny showing Sully the cash. Probably stuffed in a bag, bundled together. The money was real after all. Jimmy wondered if it was the twenty-six thousand dollars. Would Sonny go to all this trouble for just twenty-six thousand? Jimmy didn't think so. Sully's story about his dead mom and an inheritance might have been real. He just didn't tell Jimmy the rest of the story. If Sully was placing bets on fights again, that would explain where he got the money to do it. And from the sound of it, he must have picked a winner, or groomed one. Jimmy wondered where Sully's boy was. His right hand pulsed.

"There's just one thing about this that I haven't pegged yet," Sonny said, his voice changing pitch. Must be walking around the room. Jimmy tried to imagine where Sully was in there, where Ricky and Sonny were, what good a bloody wrench would be against them, both packing for certain.

"I don't know how you found out about my fix. I suppose Buster could have come to you with it after I got him lined up, but that doesn't quite fit. Buster's a hell of a fighter, but a little vacant upstairs, you know?"

Jimmy shook his head. Buster Grant, had to be him. Jimmy sparred with him once, but not again. Kid had a right hand like a cement mixer. When Jimmy knew him, the kid was on his way to being something. Sounded like he didn't get there, though. Goddamn.

"Buster didn't set this up, someone had to come to him with it, and for the same reason I came to him. Whacked out on that shit he shoots, career flushing down the toilet because of it. Guy like that is pliable. Easily bent to a strong personality. Highly suggestible sort, as you found out. But how'd you get to him? Before Ricky puts a bullet through your head, I want you to tell me."

A silent beat passed. Jimmy edged closer to the doorway, dying to look in. Needed to know what was happening in there. If they shoot Sully, they wouldn't hang around, and here he stood with a wrench in his hands, in the open with nowhere to hide. He almost didn't realize what Ricky said at first. Not until he heard the surprise in Sonny's voice.

"What the hell is this shit?"

Jimmy peeked around the corner until he could see inside the office. He saw Sully in a chair with his back to the door, silver bands of duct tape wrapped around his body, wrists, ankles, strapped down. Sonny standing on the opposite side of a metal desk with an axe stuck in the middle of its battered top. And Ricky with a stainless steel Smith & Wesson 686 leveled at Sonny's head.

"This shit is what it is."

Sonny spluttered, kept his hands at his sides. Sweat drenched his pink dress shirt in dark circles at the armpits and around the neck.

"You sorry son of a bitch." Sonny shook his head. "I'd like to say I should have known, but damn, Ricky. I thought you were loyal."

Ricky said, "Loyalty goes only so far, Sonny. I ain't spending the rest of my life following you around. Playing this small-time bullshit for you. Pick up the bag and toss it on the floor at my feet."

Sully strained against his bonds. "Cut this shit off me and I'll get it myself," he said.

Ricky ignored him, locked in on Sonny, who looked from Sully to Ricky, said, "So you're going to fall in with a loser like him?"

"I'm not in with anyone but me. Toss the bag over. Not gonna tell you again."

Sonny reached down behind the desk, lifted a leather travel bag from the floor. Zipped it shut and tossed it over Sully's head. It landed at Ricky's feet. He bent over and picked it up, never taking his eyes or his gun off Sonny. Jimmy couldn't tell if Sonny was armed, but assumed he was. Had a gun on him somewhere and Ricky would know that.

"There you go, you're a rich fucking man," Sonny said. "Now what are you going to do? Head down to South Beach and party?"

Sully strained harder against the tape. "Ricky, come on, what is this shit? Cut me loose, man."

Ricky, still backing for the door, almost to the threshold, said, "What I do now will be none of your concern." Added with a smile in his voice, "Trust me."

Jimmy realized Ricky was going to shoot them both. A room full of crooks double-crossing each other. It would have been poetic if he wasn't stuck in the fucking middle of it. He had to do something. He decided that he wasn't going to let this ape shoot his friend, no matter how much the prick deserved it. He wanted Sully for himself.

Jimmy crouched in the doorway, Ricky two strides away and inching closer. Sonny's eyes fell on Jimmy, shock on his face for a second before he quickly looked back up at Ricky, who noticed it. The big man turned, his gun coming with him. By the time he saw Jimmy coming at him, Jimmy was already bringing the wrench down on his face. Jimmy swung with his left hand, used the right to block Ricky's gun aside, away from his body. Ricky fired a round that punched through the office wall. So loud Jimmy thought his head would explode. So loud he couldn't hear the wrench connect with Ricky's face. The bloody clench jaw smashed into Ricky's nose, mashed it flat against his face, showered Jimmy with a spray of blood.

Ricky pitched forward, going down hard. Behind the desk, Sonny already had his gun out of his waist at the small of his back. Brought it up fast, a flash of flat black in the shape of a Walther P99, same gun Sonny shoved in Jimmy's face two years ago before, telling Jimmy he wasn't going to kill him.

Jimmy got low and spun away from Ricky's crumpling form, rammed his shoulder into the doorframe as he dove out of the office. Sonny's rounds were a much duller noise, like hearing underwater. Jimmy felt the air sizzle as one skipped off the metal workbench and past his face and then he was behind the workbench. Couldn't see to the back of the office anymore, just a sliver through the junk under the bench. Ricky in the doorway on one knee, his Smith and Wesson pressed barrel-down on the floor, holding him up, his left hand holding his face. Blood squirted between his fingers, splashed on the bare concrete floor in front of him. He squinted at Jimmy, tears streaming down his cheeks. He brought the S&W up but Jimmy heard another pop from the Walther and Ricky's forehead erupted. A jagged flap of skin and skull flew away, a geyser of blood spraying out as Ricky fell dead. The 686, stainless steel finish with a hard, black Hogue rubber grip, skittered forward.

Jimmy didn't think, just reacted. Reached out with the wrench and hooked the jaw inside the gun's trigger guard and pulled it toward him. Another round from the Walther struck the wrench, yanked it from his hand. He reached with his gnarled right hand and snagged the Smith & Wesson, pulled it to him the rest of the way as another round skipped off the floor, peppered Jimmy with tiny, hot pieces of concrete shrapnel. He wiped at his face and his hand came away bloody, but didn't know if it was his own or from Ricky's crushed nose.

Jimmy peered through the tangle of discarded and mismatched engine parts and tools piled up below the workbench. He saw inside the office, the far wall that had been out of sight when he had been crouched on the other side of the doorway. A body lay against that wall. A black man, with chunks of duct tape hanging from him like flayed skin, a pair of filthy blue satin boxing trunks, blue patent leather boots. His face was obscured by his left arm, but Jimmy knew it was Buster Grant, and his right hand screamed at him. He wondered if Buster got it as bad, but decided that he must have gotten much worse. Jimmy didn't realize at first that Sonny was talking to him and he strained to hear over the high-pitched whine inside his head.

"What's that Sonny? You said you're gonna throw your gun out here and beg for my mercy?"

Jimmy heard him this time, laughing like he was truly amused. "I don't think that's going to happen, Jimmy. I would ask you to do the same, but you're not that stupid. I mean, just the fact that you're here with this fuck up you call a friend proves that you're stupid, but I know you're not *that* stupid."

Jimmy looked through the junk under the bench, hoped to find a thick chunk of iron he could use for a shield. He found nothing that he was confident would stop a .357 round from that Walther.

Sonny shouted from the office, "I would say we're evenly matched here, you with Ricky's Smith and Wesson and all, but I'm wondering something."

"You're wondering if I'll just put one in your head so you can go fast, rather than pumping one into your gut so you die nice and slow and painful."

More laughter. "No, not quite. I'm wondering, what with your right hand not what it once was, if you can shoot that great big gun with your left. It's a hard thing to squeeze off an accurate shot, under duress, using your non-dominant hand, and with such a heavy weapon."

"You're about to find out. You ready?"

"Jimmy, you don't sound very confident. You're

talking tough but I can hear the worry in your voice. You'll only get one shot at this. And you don't want to hit your buddy here. Right in the middle."

Sully shouted, "He's behind the desk, Jimmy. Just shoot him through the fucking desk!"

Jimmy heard a smack, metal against skin. Sully croaked in pain. Sonny must have reached across the desk and pistol-whipped him. Sully didn't say another word.

Sonny said, "Yeah, come on Jimmy. You can do it. Just jump out here and light me up."

Jimmy didn't do it. Sonny was right. He had cover and the more manageable gun. Even with a good right hand, Jimmy knew he couldn't take Sonny in this position. He needed something else. A distraction. He looked through the mess under the bench again, found a coffee can filled with nails and screws. That might work. Get Sonny ducking a hail of metal and punch a bunch of holes through that desk. And try not to hit Sully in the process, but still get lucky and catch Sonny with one of them.

That plan sucked.

Jimmy peeked around the bench, tried to catch a glimpse of Sonny. A round banged off the leg of the bench, just missed Jimmy's nose. He scrambled back, heart slamming against his ribs.

"You OK, Jimmy? Did I get you?"

Jimmy grabbed the can of screws and got his feet under him. The plan sucked but he didn't have a better one. He took a deep breath, then took a second one. Thought about Annie and their baby and wondered what would happen to them. If he could get to the front door, he would, just get the fuck out of there and don't stop until he was holding Annie, but that wasn't happening. He had to cross in front of the office to get out the front door. If he wanted to see them again, he had to kill Sonny.

And even if he had no one to go back home to, Jimmy realized he wouldn't leave there until Sonny was dead. This had to end now.

Jimmy held the near-full coffee can in his right hand, pulled back the hammer on the 686, and got ready to go, but movement in the office stopped him. He watched the broken fighter in the back corner, Buster Grant, struggle to his knees. The kid was covered in blood and looked dead, but he pushed himself to his feet using a sledgehammer for leverage. Jimmy waited for Sonny to shoot him, but Sonny just kept talking.

"How about it, Jimmy? We need to get this over with already. If you think you can wait it out until the cops show up, you're wrong. Listen hard, no distant sirens getting closer. Cops don't come out to this neighborhood, and even if anyone heard these shots, they won't be dialing nine-one-one. This shit is a way of life out here. So it's just down to you and me and I'm ready to collect my money and move the fuck on."

Buster wobbled on loose knees, but he bent down and gripped the sledgehammer in the middle of handle and staggered forward. Jimmy caught sight of Buster's right hand, or rather where his right hand should have been, and his stomach dropped. Buster hefted the sledge, turned to get his whole body behind the swing. Jimmy set the can down and moved for the office door.

Sonny was rising from behind the desk, his head swiveling around to face Buster. The sledge connected as Jimmy came through the door. Sonny's head, his whole body, spun around, his jaw sideways, the sound of it shattering nearly as loud as a gunshot. Jimmy raised the Smith & Wesson, but didn't use it. The Walther dropped from Sonny's hand, clattered onto the desk. Sonny dropped to the floor and didn't move.

Buster let go of the sledgehammer and fell against the wall, slid down to the floor. Jimmy reached for the Walther and stopped. He stood and stared for a long time at the smashed boxing glove, lying in blood, a jagged bone sticking out of the wrist. He looked over at Buster, who sat watching him back. Buster's eyes fell to Jimmy's right hand, the fingers curled in toward the palm. It pulsed with old pain.

Sully mumbled, blood trailing from his split lips in strings. Jimmy walked over to him. His friend looked up, smiled meekly.

"Good job, man," Sully slurred. "You got his ass."

Without thinking about it, Jimmy raised the Smith & Wesson, pressed the barrel against Sully's temple. The hammer was still down. Sully's eyes widened. He was fully conscious now.

"Alright, man," he said. "OK. Alright, JP."

Jimmy's finger twitched against the trigger. The slightest squeeze would take care of his biggest problem for good. Paint the wall with it. Sully shut his mouth and looked straight ahead. Saw Jimmy's expression and knew that was it. Jimmy was stone-faced. Still, save for his gently rising chest. Stayed that way until Sully began to tremble. Was it fear or the ALS?

Jimmy finally spoke. "Last chance at the truth. Are you sick?"

Sully didn't look at him, just kept staring ahead. He nodded. "Yes."

"Your mom really died?"

"Yes."

"And instead of taking the money and giving it to me like you said you were, you laid down a bet with it. So you could still pay me off and have some for yourself."

Sully nodded.

"How did you get hooked up with Ricky?"

Sully swallowed. "I lied about Mom's funeral. I did come back for it. Heard her will read by the lawyer. Went to a bar after. Ricky was following me. Found out I was back, was going to blow my head off. Said he wasn't told to do it, but just wanted to because he didn't like me. I told him about the will. About the money I had coming. He thought about it and had a better idea."

Buster, voice thick with pain, said, "I was supposed to meet the lawyer here. Didn't say nothing about none of y'all."

Sully shook his head. "You weren't supposed to know about us. Ricky was going to shoot you and Sonny both. I figured I was going to get it, too, but what the fuck was I supposed to do?"

Jimmy pressed the gun into Sully's head. "You knew that and you still brought me along?"

"I thought I could tell you what was what. That you'd help me out, back me up in here. But then you found me in that gas station bathroom. I thought you were gonna run me down for real. I knew I made a mistake bringing you, but I figured you would just leave like you said you would."

Jimmy breathed, eased up with the gun. Thumbed the hammer up and held it at his side. Sully looked at him, tremors getting worse. He tried to smile. "I always could count on you, Jimmy. No matter what. And look how this turned out? We got the money, right?"

Buster said, "Whatchu mean look how it turned out. You see my hand on the fuckin' desk there, asshole?" He struggled to stand again, pushed himself up with his back to the wall. Buster held up his charred stump, the blackened flesh cracked and seeping. "You think this shit turned out good, motherfucker?"

Jimmy looked from Buster's stump down to Sonny on the floor. Sonny's eyes, wide and running with tears, watched them. Darted from Jimmy to Buster and back. He blinked and Jimmy moved around the desk. He pulled Sonny up by the shirt and shoved him into the empty chair behind the desk. Sonny groaned in agony, his jaw slack, canted to the left and hung crooked.

Buster lurched toward Sonny, gripped his ruined jaw in his remaining hand and squeezed. Sonny screamed.

"Look who's still with us," Buster said.

Jimmy patted Sonny down, felt the breast pocket of his pink shirt. Looked in the desk drawers, rummaged through papers until he came up with a box cutter. He flicked the blade out and walked back to Sully. Once Sully was free of the tape, Jimmy tossed the box cutter to Buster and said, "Keep an eye on him."

He slipped the 686 into the back of his pants and plucked the Walther off the desk. Released the clip, checked it, re-inserted it and pulled back the slide. Jimmy walked out of the office and scanned the workbench. He didn't find what he wanted and picked up the coffee can of screws and nails, dumped it out on the desk in the office.

Jimmy said to Sully, "Go out there and find me a hammer."

Sully shuffled away and Jimmy pushed the pile of fasteners around. He plucked out a four-inch deck screw and a crooked gutter spike. Sully returned with a hammer, handed it to Jimmy who tucked it under his arm. He nodded at the axe still stuck in the desk. "Pull that out of the way."

Sully did, rocking it back and forth until it came free.

Jimmy said to Sonny, "Hands out flat on the desk and keep them there."

Sonny hesitated and Buster squeezed his jaw again. Sonny shrieked and slapped his hands on the desk on each side of Buster's glove.

Jimmy said, "Hold him down."

Sully got on one side of Sonny and Buster on the other and they leaned on him, gripping his arms. Jimmy held the seven-inch long gutter spike in his face. "If you move, I'll use this to nail your ballsack to that chair. Understand?"

Sonny nodded and winced at the pain the effort caused him. Jimmy put the Walther in his front waist band, held the hammer with his left hand and placed the gutter spike in the middle of Sonny's arm, just behind the wrist. With one swing, Jimmy drove the spike through Sonny's arm between the radius and ulna bones, down into the desk. Sonny squealed and bucked against Sully and Buster, but Jimmy continued to hammer the spike into the desk until the head was flush against Sonny's skin. He jerked against it, but his arm didn't move and brought on fresh screams. Buster came around and helped Sully hold the other arm down and Jimmy repeated the process with the deck screw until both of Sonny's hands were pinned to the desk at the wrists. Sully and Buster backed away.

Jimmy stood and stared at Sonny, who quivered and whined, looking up at him with his crooked jaw. Jimmy held the hammer up, showed it to him, and slowly transferred it from his left hand to his right. Water dripped somewhere in the room and Buster looked down at the floor.

"Motherfucker's pissing himself." He leaned over and whispered into Sonny's ear, "You one filthy nigga."

Sonny cried.

Jimmy swung the hammer. He ignored the ache in his hand, and eventually, it went away. He brought the hammer down over and over onto Sonny's right hand. Splinters of bone split through skin. Blood flung off the hammer in ropes, painting the wall, the ceiling, himself. He stopped swinging when the deck screw finally pulled free. Sonny slipped from the chair, ruined right hand held close to his chest. The longer gutter spike held fast, didn't budge. Sonny dangled from it, his knees on the floor, left arm dislocated at the shoulder, as crooked as his face.

Jimmy handed the hammer to Buster.

Buster swung it, over and over, until he collapsed, fell against the desk and dropped to the floor. Sonny's left hand was ground meat. He wheezed in and out, a wet rasp in his chest, his throat shredded from screaming.

Jimmy picked the hammer up and Sully stepped toward him, his hand held out for it. Jimmy looked at Sully's hand and came at him with the hammer. Sully scrambled away. He fell over the chair and landed on his back, hands held out, screaming at Jimmy to stop.

"The fuck you think you're doing," Jimmy said.

"I don't know," Sully said. "I don't know what I'm doing. Dammit, Jimmy, don't do me like this."

Jimmy ground his teeth together. "I'm not. Goddammit, I want to, but I'm not." Tears burned his eyes and he wiped at them, lowered the hammer to his side. "You fuckin' asshole, Sully."

Jimmy threw the hammer at Sully. It struck him, heavy in the chest.

"You don't get payback from anybody you piece of shit. You owe, Sully."

A new voice from outside the office said, "Starting with me."

Another deafening gun shot inside the tight office and Sully's brains blew out the side of his head, slapped against the paneled wall. He dropped sideways, dead before he hit the floor.

Jimmy staggered back and looked at the two men coming through the door into the office. A middle-aged guy with long hair and a goatee, a nine-millimeter pointed at Jimmy's head. The second guy was older, salt and pepper hair and closely trimmed beard. Thick, black-framed Harry Carey glasses like Coke bottles.

The old guy said, "And now, Sully, you don't owe me no more." The old guy stared down at Sully, hocked up phlegm and spit it at the body. His eyes moved to the desk, the mush that was Sonny hand, the rest of his arm still pegged there by the spike. Looked at Buster's glove and down to Buster on the floor, breathing heavily on his side, watching them. His eyes finally fell on Jimmy. The old man's face brightened.

"I'll be damned," he said. "If it ain't Jimmy fuckin' Paradise." He nudged the shooter and said, "Mick, you remember Jimmy, don't you?"

Mick nodded, never moved that nine from Jimmy's face, and said, "Yeah, Jimmy Two Tickets to Paradise. Course I do. How's things, Jimmy?"

Jimmy shrugged, realized his hands were up. Licked his lips and said, "Things have been better."

The old man said, "You remember me, don't you Jimmy?"

Jimmy thought for a moment and said, "Yeah, now I do. Mr. Sims, right?"

Sims smiled. "Sure, you remember."

Sonny groaned, tried to pull himself up, fell back again and cried out as the spike dug against his arm bones.

Sims walked around the desk and looked down at Sonny, shook his head and scratched his beard. "Jesus, what a mess."

He looked back up at Jimmy. "This is not how we do things." He pointed at Jimmy's hand. "That," he said, "is not how we do things. You know the reason people don't respect boxing no more?"

Jimmy had his opinions, none of which he cared to share at that moment. Instead he just shook his head.

"Because of guys like this," Sims said, pointing down at Sonny. "Because it's full of crooks who think they're hotshots. Think just because they put a few fights together it gives them the right to throw a couple. Too many sonsabitches trying to make a fast buck in this sport, but that ain't the way to do it. You know what I mean, don't you."

It wasn't a question, just statement of fact. Jimmy sure as shit knew what he meant and nodded at the old man.

"A boxer's got to train hard," Sims continued. "He's got to give up everything else and devote himself to the science if he wants to be something. Boxing is the American way. It's a sport that even the lowest, dumbest bastard around can succeed in, if he's willing to put in his time. Do the hard work that's necessary." Sims pointed at Sonny. "Guys like this, they don't put in the time and pay their dues. You have to earn respect. My old grandfather used to say, 'Any man thinks he's entitled to your respect will never deserve it.' That old man was right."

He squatted down and pulled Sonny's head up by the hair. Looked at his face, at his broken jaw, and grimaced. "You've gotten everything you deserved, you fuckin' half Wop greaseball piece of shit. You've got no respect for this sport and no respect for the people who run it, and now we're going to have all manner of heat come down on us because of this. Illinois State Athletic Commission is already talking about an investigation. I'm too old for this nonsense."

Sims let go of Sonny's head and walked around the desk to Buster. "Son, you stole from me," he said. "You could have been a hell of a fighter, but you let that shit get a hold of you, and now look at you." Sims shook his head and glanced at Mick.

Mick turned and put a bullet in Buster's chest, a second one in his head. Jimmy shrank back against the wall, his hands still up. Mick moved around behind the desk and shot Sonny in the head. The wheezing stopped and the room was quiet save for the ringing in Jimmy's head. Blue smoke drifted toward the ceiling.

Sims said to no one in particular, "I think it might be time to get out of this business for good." Jimmy thought he might have still been talking to the dead men littered around his feet. Sims sighed and turned for the door.

Mick gestured at Jimmy with his gun. "What about this one?"

Sims looked over his shoulder at Mick then over to Jimmy. He said, "Everyone in this room tried to steal from me but Jimmy." He walked up to Jimmy and pointed at his gnarled hand. "I had beef with the rest, but this one? He's just a fighter. Right, Jimmy?"

"Yeah. Right."

Sims stared at Jimmy's hand and shook his head. "I feel bad what happened to you, kid. Never should have gone like that. There's no place in boxing for people like these. It's no wonder people don't take the sport seriously no more. This was a long time coming for Sonny, and for your pal Sully, too."

Jimmy said nothing. Just waited for the old man to change his mind. He didn't.

"I always liked you, Jimmy, because you were respectful. You worked hard, you did your job. You just got unlucky when it came to your friends. Maybe if we had a few more guys like you around, I wouldn't be thinking about an early retirement. Where you gonna go now, kid?"

"Home. I'm going home now."

Sims nodded. "Good. You take care of yourself."

Sims walked out of the office and Mick followed, stooped to pick up the satchel lying next to Ricky. Unzipped it, checked inside, closed it up again. He left without another glance at Jimmy, who slipped down the wall until his ass hit the cool concrete floor. He held his head in his hands as the front door banged shut.

A second later, the rattle of automatic weapon fire out on the street. Rounds slammed through the cheap sheet metal outer walls of the body shop, punched holes through the paneled interior walls of the office. Splinters and plaster showered onto Jimmy, face down with his arms over his head. One long burst of fire, over a dozen rounds at least until Jimmy figured the weapon was empty. Then quiet for a long time. Jimmy lay there, breathing, listening. Waiting for the gunman outside to reload. To come in and finish him off. He didn't move until the high buzz in his ears dissipated and he could make out the distant whine of sirens.

Jimmy crawled over to the door and looked out into the shop. Nothing moved except a puddle of oil spreading across the floor. Smell of fuel in there now, everything riddled with bullet holes, leaking fluid. The grill was tipped over, a steaming circle in its metal side, ash-covered charcoals spilled out over the floor. He pulled Sonny's Walther from his waistband and went to the door, watched the puddle advance toward the coals.

Jimmy opened the front door and looked outside. It was quiet. The sirens were moving away from him, their Doppler warble fading. He scanned the street a few more seconds then tucked the Walther back into his pants. He reached around and pulled Ricky's 686 out, used his shirt to wipe down the handle and trigger guard, turned and tossed it back into the puddle of oily gas. He took a breath and walked out onto the sidewalk.

Sims and Mick lay heaped together, also riddled with holes and leaking fluid. The bag of money between them on the ground. Jimmy dug into his pocket, pulled out his keys, looked up and saw a black man standing in the street, an AK-47 in his hands.

"Is that Jimmy Paradise?"

Jimmy squinted through the darkness, the sliver of moonlight above not enough to make the guy out. He tried to keep the rattle out of his voice.

"Who's that?"

The guy stepped closer until Jimmy recognized the face. He struggled to come up with a name.

"Buster dead, ain't he?"

"Yeah, he's dead." It finally came to him. Mitch Sampson. Buster Grant's uncle. He remembered the old guy from his early days training at Windy City Gym. He was a tough old guy, but he wasn't a gangster.

"They shoot him?"

"Yes." Jimmy nudged Mick's leg and said, "This one right here." He didn't plan to tell Mitch what Sonny had done to his nephew's hand.

"Anybody left but you?"

"No."

"I ain't expect to see you here."

"I didn't expect to be here."

"Your buddy Sully got you into it?"

"Yeah. My buddy Sully. What are you going to do with that AK, Mitch?"

Mitch looked at the rifle. "This just something I brought back from 'Nam with me. A souvenir."

Jimmy waited, wondered if he was going to die now.

Mitch said, "I ain't shot this thing in over thirty years. Didn't think I'd ever have to again. You ain't got to worry. I'm not gonna shoot you, Jimmy. Don't have no more bullets no how."

Jimmy crouched, slow, picked up the bag, held it out to Mitch. "You come for this?"

Mitch shook his head. "Nope. I got what I came for."

The sirens grew louder again, but still several blocks off. Mitch said, "You best be gettin' on then. Take that with you. I don't want to see it no more."

"What are you going to do, Mitch?"

"Me? I'm going home."

Mitch turned and walked to his car, early 2000s Mercury Cougar. He got in, looking more like a man leaving work for the day than one who just shot two men. Mitch set the rifle on the floor behind his front seat and drove away. Jimmy crossed the street. He tossed the bag of money behind the truck's bench seat and did the same.

THE NEXT DAY

Ray Nichols pulled into the parking lot of the Jefferson Estates apartment complex, drove to the east end of the first row of buildings, and parked in the last spot. He turned off the engine and sat drumming his fingers against the steering wheel. It got hot fast inside the Caprice and he mopped away sweat with his sleeve.

He didn't expect to find anything there. He'd already been to Crestline, where the kid worked. Talked to Vic, the drunk who called in the tip about Anthony Sullivan. Saw it on the news and couldn't believe it, he'd just talked to that guy the other night, was in some bar over in LaPorte County, Indiana, and now the guy was dead. It was the damndest thing.

Nichols visited the coffee shop in the toll road rest area, but the girl, Annie, she hadn't been to work in a week. Her boss asked Nichols, should he see her, to tell her she was fired. Nichols told him to go fuck himself. The guy, he didn't like that. Called Nichols an asshole. Nichols didn't argue with him.

He got out and walked to the office. Checked in with the manager, an immense woman in a housecoat, cigarette protruding from her face and one eye squinted against the smoke curling around her head. She looked like a pirate.

"Have you seen them lately?"

The woman shook her head, dropping ash across the countertop separating them. "Not since last week," she said. "Paid their next two months' rent and that's the last I seen of 'em."

Nichols smiled, couldn't help himself. He said, "Arrr, thank ye, matey."

He left the office and walked back to the last apartment building. Climbed the steps to the second floor, went to the last door at the end of the walkway. He knocked and waited and when no one answered, he grabbed the handrail to his right and the doorframe of the neighboring apartment to his left and kicked the door in. The lock was solid, but the door was a cheap piece of shit.

Nichols walked in, looked around the corner, checked the tiny kitchen area, his hands shoved in his pockets. He wasn't concerned. They weren't there. He checked the bedroom in back and the bathroom, flipping lights on, flipping them off again. He strolled back toward the door but stopped when he saw the leather satchel on the couch.

Nichols sat down on the threadbare cushions and looked at the satchel. It was a bit old-fashioned, a zipper top that accordioned out when you opened it. The zipper was already undone. He leaned over and looked inside the bag. Saw a note. He pulled a pair of latex gloves from the breast pocket of his short-sleeve dress shirt. Cost only ten bucks on sale at Target. He plucked the note out and sat back. It had been typed on a computer, printed out on a laser printer, cheap copy paper. It read:

To the cop or anyone else who happens to find this, an offer: Take what's in this bag and look the other way. We're long gone and you won't find us.

Nichols peered in the bag again and smiled. He reached inside and pulled out the bundle of cash, held together by a rubber band. All hundreds, he counted 50 of them. He continued reading:

If you're not a cop, then I guess you're not going to be happy with this. But it's the best you're going to get. As I mentioned, we're already long gone. You won't find us. You'll just have to trust me on this.

Have a nice day.

Nichols smiled again. It was a nice touch. He flipped through the bills, counted them once more. He stood and slipped the money into the front pocket of his slacks, wadded up the note and tossed it back in the bag. He zipped it shut and left, did his best to close the door behind him. On his way to his car, he tossed the bag and his gloves into a dumpster.

He opened the Caprice's glove box, set the wad of money inside, removed a Tracfone and turned it on. The box for the phone was in a bag on the floor behind the front seat, paid for with cash. The receipt went in the trashcan just outside the door of the 7-11. Once the phone powered up, he punched in the number from memory and listened. It rang five times before the girl answered.

"Hello?"

"Annie, don't hang up. It's your father."

Silence. He waited one heartbeat to see if she would cut him off. When she didn't, he kept going.

"Just hear me out, OK? I heard through the grapevine that I'm going to be a grandpa. That got me thinking. I know we left things in a bad way. I have some making up to do, to both of you kids. I'm getting older now and starting to see things a little different. I'm done being a cop. I quit today. I thought maybe I could try to be a dad now since I never did much of that before. Maybe try my hand at being a grandpa, too. I was hoping I could come and visit with you two and get started on that. If you told me where you and Jimmy are living now, I could—"

The line went dead.

Nichols smiled. He knew she wouldn't tell him anything. Now that she knew he was on to them, she'd toss her cell and kick herself for not doing so sooner.

He didn't have to do it, but calling would just add to the fun of tracking them down. It put him in the right mood. He hummed as he dropped the car in gear and drove off.

Acknowledgements:

Big thanks go to Jeremy Robert Johnson, David Barbee, and Chris Masciangelo, the guys who saw this book before anyone else, took the time to read it, and gave me their much-appreciated advice and encouragement. Shout-outs to Gabino Iglesias and Caris O'Malley, great friends and the two people in this world who may have read every single thing I've written. Finally, special thanks to Tom Piccirilli, who doesn't know me from Adam but is a great inspiration, as are you, J.

ABOUT THE AUTHOR:

Steve Lowe writes some odd shit, but he's also a freelance sports writer. He interviewed a naked heavyweight once and continues to talk about it to this day. He's got a website but it's probably better if you just holla at ya boy on Twitter - @Steve_Lowe